MORE PRAISE FOR TIM CHAMPLIN!

BLOOD MONEY

"Because of the bitterness remaining from Reconstruction, and the bitterness of this family feud, hatreds are going to flare into killings. This is not just a treasure hunt. This is deadly serious business…as you found out the other day."

"I don't want anything to happen to Nellie," Rasmussen said.

"I don't, either. I suspected you were sweet on her."

"She told me she was disgusted with the whole business and wants nothing to do with it. But, by accident of birth, she is part of it. Tried to convince her to leave here and start another life, but she said she couldn't bring herself to run away."

"Sometimes our loyalties can be the death of us."

Rasmussen pondered the wisdom of this statement. Uncle Bill had saved his life. He owed the man everything; he couldn't just walk away.

"I'll work with you." He held out his hand. "Tell me the plan." Committing himself, he felt the stab of danger in his gut. Loyalty to this mission might, indeed, be the death of them.

COLD CACHE

Tim Champlin

LEISURE BOOKS NEW YORK CITY

For my sister Peggy,
whose sense of humor overcomes everything.

A LEISURE BOOK®

June 2009

Published by special arrangement with Golden West Literary Agency.

Dorchester Publishing Co., Inc.
200 Madison Avenue
New York, NY 10016

ISBN 10: 0-8439-6030-2
ISBN 13: 978-0-8439-6030-3
E-ISBN: 978-1-4285-0686-2

The name "Leisure Books" and the stylized "L" with design are trademarks of Dorchester Publishing Co., Inc.

Printed in the United States of America.

10 9 8 7 6 5 4 3 2 1

Visit us on the web at www.dorchesterpub.com.

COLD CACHE

Chapter One:
Windsor, Ontario

June 2, 1890

Kent Rasmussen was leaving the North-West Mounted Police. He'd spent the past eight years wearing the red in frontier provinces—enough to satisfy all his youthful illusions, and adult expectations. At the urging of his comrades-in-arms, he'd seriously considered reënlistment to make the Canadian service his career. But a severely frostbitten foot suffered six months earlier during a manhunt southwest of Old Wives Lake had persuaded him to seek another line of work at age thirty-seven, still reasonably young and with all his appendages. Once he'd made a firm decision, he forged ahead, casting aside all doubts and second thoughts.

Kent breathed deeply of the fresh air, looped his horse's reins around the rail in front of the branch bank in Windsor, and stepped up onto the boardwalk. Although full summer was probably bursting forth farther south, a chill north breeze still tempered the hazy sunshine here. He stopped to squint across the river toward the low, jumbled buildings of Detroit. Although indistinguishable from buildings on this side of the border, they represented the

United States of America—his home. He was returning after eight long years.

A light drumming of heels on the boardwalk
swung his attention to a young woman approaching, dressed in a hooded traveling cape, and carrying a small leather bag. As she slowed by the door,
Rasmussen swept off his stiff-brim hat and reached
for the doorknob. She tossed back her hood, chest-
nut hair cascading to her shoulders, and flashed him
a brief smile. "Thank you, sir."

She passed in, trailing a faint, eloquent fragrance.
What was it? Lilac? Jasmine? He couldn't distinguish
the scent of one toilet water from another. Sensibili-
ties dulled by too many years of smelling pipe smoke
and pine trees. He'd have to catch up on the finer
things of life, he reflected, swinging the door shut
behind him. Pausing in the shaded interior, he felt
several pairs of eyes turn in his direction. Too little
contact with civilized society made him feel conspicuous in his red uniform. He approached a teller's
cage and slipped a money clip from his pocket. Un-
folding a stack of bills, he pushed them across the
oak counter.

"Convert this to American currency," he said to
the slim, black-suited clerk. The stack represented a
month's pay plus a small separation bonus.

"Right you are, Constable," the teller replied, ignoring the sergeant's stripes on Rasmussen's sleeves.
"There'll be a slight fee for that."

"OK." Rasmussen nodded, beginning to realize
that everything in civilian life had its cost. No longer
would the force provide all his needs. Just another
adjustment he'd have to make after long months in
the field. Attached to isolated outposts, he and his
messmates seldom had had use for cash, except to

settle up small wagers on pay day, or to buy tobacco and other personal items from the sutler.

While the teller counted the money and searched his cash drawer, Rasmussen found himself distracted by the voice of the young woman at the next window.

"Why should I have to see the bank manager?" she demanded. "Can't you handle this transaction? Isn't everything in order?"

The balding teller's eyes darted nervously. "Of course, miss." He smoothed some sort of document on the counter and lowered his voice. In the quiet atmosphere, Rasmussen had no trouble overhearing his words. "It's just that the branch manager must approve a withdrawal of this size. And it's customary to issue a bank draft for large sums."

"I don't want your paper," she replied. "I want it all in United States currency." She set her small leather grip on the counter. "Your bank has been earning money on this account for twenty-five years, but now you're saying I can't have it in cash? Here's my authorization."

"But, miss. . . ."

"OK, if this is too big for you, where's the manager?" she asked, obviously annoyed at the timid clerk.

"One moment." The teller disappeared toward the back.

She took the small black satchel and stepped away from the barred window, biting at the corner of her lip.

With a sidelong glance, Rasmussen studied her from beneath his eyelids. She wasn't much over five feet tall, but the girl moved in a confident way and her sharp profile emphasized a perky, defiant air.

"Three hundred forty-seven dollars and thirty cents." The clerk's voice brought Rasmussen back to his own business. The teller carefully counted out the large, crisp greenbacks. "The exchange rate is a bit in your favor just now."

"Thanks," Rasmussen said, folding and thrusting the bills into his silver money clip—a departing gift from the men of his regiment.

As he turned toward the door, the woman looked up and seemed really to notice him for the first time. Her bold look showed no apologies for making a scene. Their eyes locked briefly, and he nodded. She didn't change expression, but her gaze swept down his six foot, two inch frame, encompassing the red and blue dress uniform, the white lanyard cord from his neck to the long-barreled Colt holstered at his side, then down to his shiny black boots. It took her only seconds to size him up, yet he felt his smooth-shaven cheeks reddening as he dragged his attention from her and reached for the door handle. If eyes are windows of the soul, he felt his soul had just been searched and found wanting.

Outside in the sun and fresh air, he shook off the feeling and donned his hat. Being around white women, instead of Indian squaws, was another part of civilized living to which he'd have to become re-accustomed.

He mounted and started his short ride back to the transfer depot on the edge of town. Then he recalled his lack of civilian clothes and reined in at the nearest general store. Socks, ankle high shoes, canvas pants and belt, two shirts, and saddlebags to carry them in would be enough for now. He added a corduroy jacket and a brown felt hat, paying for the lot with some Canadian money he'd retained for emergencies.

An hour later, he was signing forms and processing out from the Mounted Police depot. A clerical error was discovered involving his time in service. While clerks pored over his personnel folder, Rasmussen changed into the new drab civilian clothing, turned in his uniform, gear, and revolver to the supply sergeant, then led his mount to the stable. He'd said farewell to former comrades a week earlier before riding away from his post in Saskatchewan. His good-byes to long-time friends remained painful. It was over and he was eager to sever the last ties and be gone.

Yet the hours dragged on, officialdom not wanting to release him until his record was completely in order. He became impatient to catch the last ferry to Detroit. But four o'clock had come and gone before the error was found and rectified. The officer in charge finally signed his discharge.

He tucked away the official certificate and took off at a fast walk to the waterfront, three miles away, forgetting he'd not broken in his stiff new shoes. By the time he arrived at the dock, the frost damaged toes on his right foot burned from unaccustomed walking. To his disgust, the last ferry for Detroit had left fifteen minutes earlier. Gazing across the water at Michigan, he sighed deeply. What would another day matter? Flinging the saddlebags over one shoulder, he turned back toward town and, an hour later, checked in at the Mirrott Hotel for the night.

At 7:15 that evening, the long summer daylight still flooded through the windows when he settled himself at a table in the hotel dining room. He finally relaxed, relieved by a shave and a good soak and scrub in a bathhouse down the street. His stomach growled at the aroma of fried steak. He hadn't eaten in twelve hours.

He placed his order as an attractive waitress in a white shirtwaist poured him coffee. With a good meal and a night's sleep, he'd be ready to start his new life. Shifting in his chair, he crossed an ankle over his knee, and slipped off his shoe to massage his damaged toes through his sock. The few patrons of the dining room didn't give him a second glance and he leaned back, enjoying the soft contact of the new-smelling cotton shirt against his skin. Mounted policemen always seemed to draw attention in public places. He enjoyed being anonymous.

He slipped his shoe back on and rested his elbows on the table, staring into his coffee cup. What would his new life be like? After deciding not to reenlist, he'd been unable to imagine life outside the Mounted Police. Tomorrow he'd take the train to Chicago, then on to southern Minnesota where his widowed mother lived with his older sister. Beyond that— what? He had little money to begin again since he'd sent most of his pay home to keep up his mother and sister. Maybe they'd been right not to sell the small farm and move to town as he'd suggested. He had no regrets at this point, but felt as he had when he'd enlisted in the North-West Mounted Police as a twenty-nine year old rookie. The clock's pendulum was swinging, and he wouldn't have time for too many new beginnings, so he'd best make the most of this one.

Drawing a deep breath, he looked out the window at the red disk of sun sinking through the haze in the west. A rustle of skirts interrupted and he looked up, expecting the waitress with his food.

"If you're eating alone, may I join you?"

The young woman from the bank stared down at him.

It took him only a second to cover his surprise. "Of course. Sit down." By the time he collected himself and rose to hold her chair, she had seated herself.

"You're the Mountie I saw at the bank," she stated before he could introduce himself.

He nodded.

"Where's your uniform?"

Nothing subtle or indirect about this woman, he thought. His first impression had been accurate.

"I'm no longer in the Mounted Police."

"Oh?" She arched her fine eyebrows. "Just since this morning?"

"That's right." He nodded. "I'm now an ordinary citizen, like 'most everyone else." He liked her forthright manner. Here was a solitary woman who was no shrinking violet. Then, for a moment he wondered—could he be so naïve as not to recognize a prostitute when he saw one? Why else would she boldly seek out a perfect stranger? Be leery of this one, he told himself. He'd end the conversation when his food arrived. "Did you resolve your problem with the bank?" he asked, turning the conversation to her.

"Yes, I did." She smiled, showing even, white teeth. Dark hair, swept back and fastened on each side by a tortoise shell comb, framed her face nicely. She appeared even younger than she had earlier. "I reminded them it's their business to serve customers, and not the other way around. Bankers tend to form an exaggerated opinion of themselves, and they were acting in a condescending manner . . . especially since I was a woman."

And a very attractive one, he added to himself.

"That's why I need a big, strong man. I noticed the teller listened to what you said, and did it."

This caught him off balance, but he continued sipping his coffee and ignored her, not wanting to ask what she needed him for. Obviously not to get along in a world of males, since she'd handled the bank officials well enough. He hoped she would go away and let him eat in peace.

"You have any immediate plans?" she asked.

"Leaving for home in the morning," he answered politely.

"Where's that?"

"Minnesota." She was a nosy one.

"You're not Canadian, then?"

"Not by birth. I've lived here a few years."

She was silent for several seconds, sizing him up, perhaps getting ready to come to the point. Not for a moment did he think she'd just approached him to pass the time of day.

His discomfort was relieved by the welcome interruption of the waitress with a plate of smoking steak, potatoes, and peas.

"Anything else I can get you?" the waitress asked, placing a woven basket with slices of sourdough on the table.

"Only coffee."

"All that food is making me hungry," the woman across the table said. "I'll have the same."

The waitress nodded and withdrew.

Rasmussen began to regret he'd invited her to join him. He wasn't skilled at the social graces, but she displayed a rudeness even he could recognize. Yet—

she was pretty. Perhaps she presented a distraction that was actually good for him. He'd been keeping his own counsel far too long.

"My name's Nellie Newburn," she said.

"Kent Rasmussen," he said, not offering to shake hands, as he was busy cutting his steak. "Where you from?"

She glanced around as if looking for someone eavesdropping. "Southern Missouri," she said in a lower voice.

He began to suspect her mental ship might be listing slightly.

"What brings you up north?" he asked, attempting some sort of normal conversation as he forked in a bite of steak and peas.

"The name Newburn doesn't mean anything to you, does it?" she asked, ignoring his question.

He shook his head, chewing thoughtfully. "Should it?"

"I suppose not. What about the name Clayton?"

"Nope. Can't say as I know it, either."

"Probably the two best known families in my region. Famous or infamous, depending on your point of view."

He decided to lighten up the conversation. "I've heard the notorious Missouri names of James, Dalton, and Younger. You related to them?"

"Not related, but connected in another way."

"Really?" He began to listen more closely.

But she didn't explain. Her face took on the look of a young girl about to spring a delightful surprise. "I want to hire you as my bodyguard on my return trip to Springfield, Missouri."

Apparently his manner showed he wasn't thrilled with this prospect. Her face fell. He tried quickly to make light of the whole idea, to devise some easy let-down to get rid of this Nellie Newburn.

"You can wire your family that you'll be late," she hurried on before he could reply. "It'll take only a week or two, at most, if everything goes well."

"Why do you need a bodyguard?" He didn't really want to know.

"I've only just met you, but I'm a good judge of character. You could have been thrown off the Mounted Police, for all I know, but you were wearing sergeant's stripes this morning, so you had enough good time and good character to make some rank. You're big and strong and have a police background. That's why I want to hire you. My reasons are my own for now, until you accept."

Maybe she wasn't as addled as he'd thought. She seemed articulate and a good observer. "I can't say yes or no," he hedged, "until I know if you're in some kind of danger."

"Not only would you be guarding me, but also my possessions."

"You referring to the big withdrawal you made from the bank today?"

"Yes."

"Well. . . ." He put his fork down on his plate and looked at her.

"Don't be brushing me off, Mister Rasmussen," she said impatiently, "just because you think I'm paranoid, or some scatterbrain who sat down here to tell you a wild tale." She was deadly serious now as her brown eyes held him steadily. She reached into her handbag that lay on a chair next to her and withdrew a white envelope, shoving it across the tablecloth.

He carefully opened the edge of it to see the corners of several $100 bills peeking out.

"There's five hundred dollars there. A man I know followed me here from Missouri. He's intent on killing me and taking the load of cash I have. If you see me safely to Springfield, I'll pay you another five hundred . . . a thousand dollars for less than ten days' work. That's probably the best offer you've had today."

"Nellie Newburn, you've just hired yourself a bodyguard."

Chapter Two:
En Route to Chicago

June 3, 1890

Now she had him. But, like the fella said, while noodling in muddy water under a cutbank: "I've latched onto something big and strong and slippery, but I ain't too sure what it is."

That act she'd put on, making out to be a scatterbrain, wouldn't have fooled a ten-year-old, but it was enough to hook the former Mountie. She hoped she hadn't made a mistake now that he'd agreed to work for her. She was taking an awful chance, because she really knew nothing about him. She'd found out quickly how little she knew him this morning when they were boarding the train in Detroit, after taking the ferry over.

They were shuffling through the crowd on the depot platform, filing toward their coach. Rasmussen had his saddlebags slung over one broad shoulder and her traveling bag hooked by a strap on the other. She clutched the handle of her small bag of cash, not willing to let it out of her grasp for a minute.

Glancing forward along the string of coaches, she gasped and froze. Two cars ahead, she'd glimpsed a man making for the train, favoring one leg with a distinctive limp. She'd seen that limp enough to know the man immediately.

"What's wrong?" Rasmussen asked, following her stare.

"I saw him . . . there . . . just for a second or two."

"Who?" Rasmussen was suddenly alert, tensed like a mountain lion ready to spring.

"The man who's stalking me. Johnny Clayton."

"You sure?"

"I'd know him anywhere. He's a gimp. Carries a hunk of lead in his leg where my uncle shot him eight years ago."

"Come on!" He grabbed her hand and forced his way through the surging crowd. What was he doing? "You see him now?" he rasped over his shoulder as he dragged her along.

She could see nothing around his broad frame. Pulling free of his hand, she stumbled to one side and scanned the thinning crowd. He was gone.

"No."

They stopped and let the passengers and porters flow around them.

"'Boooaardd!'" came the cry from the conductor behind them.

"Looked like Johnny was heading for one of these two coaches," she said, now none too sure of herself.

"Let's go."

She followed him up the coach steps and into the end door. The passengers were taking their seats, and he came close to her, leaning to whisper in her ear: "Walk ahead of me up and down this aisle. If you see him, reach back and touch my hand."

She nodded, her throat dry. What had she turned loose here? If they spotted Johnny, what would Rasmussen do? Throw him bodily off the train? Grab him and make a citizen's arrest? On what charge? She moved ahead along the aisle, feeling his hand in the small of her back, guiding her, letting her know he was right there. But, much to her relief, Johnny was not in that car. The train lurched into motion and they steadied themselves while it began to roll out of the station. There were three day-coaches, a diner, and a Pullman on this train and they searched all of them without seeing Clayton.

She was breathing easier by the time they found their compartment in the Pullman just forward of the caboose, and Rasmussen stashed their luggage in the overhead rack.

"I might have been mistaken," she said by way of apology for the false alarm.

"You seemed pretty sure," Rasmussen replied. "He could still be aboard, somewhere. We might've missed him. Not likely he'll stay in plain sight all the time."

She nodded, trying to recreate the moving image of the man with the limp. She was all too sure it was Johnny. "What'll you do if we find him?" she asked when her nervousness abated.

"I'll put a good scare into him, if nothing else. In this kind of situation, it's better to be offensive than defensive."

With Rasmussen, she'd gotten even more than she'd bargained for. When he took a job, he meant to do it right—not just sit back and collect his $1,000 pay. She wondered what he'd do if he knew she had enough cash in her small bag to support him for the rest of his life? Probably nothing. A girl has to put her trust in something, or somebody, and her trust was in her judgment of men. They were generally easier to read than women. And she felt sure this man was as simple and straightforward as he appeared. She was banking on the hope that he had a highly developed sense of duty.

The train picked up speed, *clacking* over the rails westward out of Detroit through the flat, wooded Michigan landscape toward Ann Arbor.

Two hours later they ate in the diner. Rasmussen said he wasn't hungry, but came along, anyway, to keep her in sight. And she reminded him the Pullman tickets they bought included all meals.

The small bag she carried everywhere was no regular satchel. It was the old-style that passengers used to carry on stagecoaches, shaped like a stiff leather cylinder, two feet long and about eight inches in diameter. It had a reinforced clasp on top that was secured with a small padlock. She kept the key in a locket around her neck.

"You don't eat much," she observed. The former Mountie was seated across the table from her, staring out at the green pastureland sliding past.

"Habit," he replied. "On long marches and campaigns, we had only what we could carry on a pack mule or in our saddlebags . . . hardtack, bacon, pemmican. Trained myself to do without," he said. "Curbing the appetite is ingrained now. If I start eating full, luxurious meals and sleeping in the comfortable beds of Pullmans, I'll get soft in no time."

"Well, I surely wouldn't want that."

It was the first time she'd seen a smile cross his face. It was a pleasant sight and she resolved to encourage more of it, and do what she could to put him at ease without causing him to lose his edge. He was here to do a job and she couldn't distract him from his natural vigilance. When he wasn't talking, his eyes were constantly roving, taking in everything— passengers, train crew, the changing view outside, but especially the other passengers.

He lapsed into silence while she continued eating the delicious roast beef and sipping red wine. How much should she tell this taciturn man about her mission to retrieve this money and return to Missouri? To her, he was a hired hand, alien to the intrigue and hatreds that had enmeshed her life and the lives of the families back home. No need to get him involved. But as they rose to leave the dining car, something happened to change her mind.

He pulled a handful of coins from his pocket to tip the white-coated waiter. Opening his hand, he selected a silver half dollar. Her eyes went wide. There, resting in his broad palm among a few coins, was an irregular shaped copper piece she recognized immediately. It was a U.S. large cent, a penny of the type that hadn't been minted since 1857. The head of Liberty had been neatly excised from the rest of the coin. The piece was well worn, but she knew it for what it was and had to swallow a couple of times before she could speak.

By then, he was moving out of the car and the time to speak was past. She followed with her bag.

When they were again seated, facing each other in their Pullman compartment, she said: "I saw what you had in your pocket."

"What was that?"

"Pull out your change again."

He obliged, holding out the contents of his pocket to her. She picked up the copper piece and turned it over. Something—probably a pin—had once been soldered to the reverse side. "Where'd you get this?"

"Belonged to my dad. He was a Copperhead during the war. I just carry it as a good luck piece. About the only thing I have to remember him by."

Apparently the Copperheads, to this man, were only a group that belonged to history. She knew similar organizations still flourished in her part of the country.

"The Copperheads were Northerners in sympathy with the Southern cause," she stated as if he were ignorant of their purpose. "They did what they could to oppose Lincoln, sabotage the Union, and end the war."

"I know. I recall him wearing this when I was a kid, pinned to his coat when he went to their meetings. My dad was always something of a maverick. He couldn't stand to go along with the crowd on anything. He gee'd when everyone else hawed." He gave a rueful smile. "Guess that's why he left on that Mormon train to Utah. He was converted by one of their missionaries, and you'd have thought he'd seen the heavenly light just over the horizon. Wanted to take my mom, sister, and me with him, but Mom was having none of it. Looking back on it, I'm sure that business of having more than one wife really set her back on her haunches. Anyway, he left, and we haven't seen him in years."

She was suddenly sorry for him. "Mister Rasmussen . . . Sergeant, I. . . ."

"It's Kent . . . and Nellie . . . as long as I'm on this job," he said.

This was the most personal conversation she'd gotten from him at one time, and she decided on the spot to reveal the entire purpose of her trip, even though he'd not pressed her to do so. Knowing him only one full day, she still instinctively felt he was worthy of her confidence. Revealing all the details might even help him do a better job protecting her. He would still not be drawn into her web, because she planned to pay him off and say good-bye when they reached Springfield.

She drew a deep breath and said: "Now listen, and I'll tell you my story."

He settled back in his seat and regarded her with steady blue eyes.

"First of all, I'm taking you smack into the middle of a feud. The Newburns and Claytons have been at each other's throats for at least a generation or two . . . since 'way before I was born."

"What about?"

"It's a long story, and I couldn't tell you how it actually got started. The basic difference was the Claytons were Free-Staters and tradesmen . . . storekeepers, blacksmiths, saloon owners, wheelwrights . . . mostly village and townspeople. My family, the Newburns, had more formal education and were farmers and slaveholders, and fairly well off. My people didn't want to give up their way of life, but knew if war came, it would disrupt everything.

"My grandfather, father, and uncles were all ruined by the war, lost their slaves, and had to sell the land they couldn't work, slaveless, for a profit. Ozark land, except for some of the coves and hollows, is forested, hilly, and rocky. The Newburns were reduced to taking menial jobs, some of them even working for the Claytons, who never let them forget how low they'd fallen. There's a lot of arrogance on both sides. . . ."

"Why didn't the Newburns go West after the war, like a lot of others did?" Rasmussen interrupted.

"Plenty of good, cheap farmland in the plains. The government even opened up the Oklahoma Territory for settlement last year."

"I know. Stubborn, I guess. Would've solved lots of problems. But there was a reason why they stayed, and I didn't learn what it was until I was thirteen." She stopped to gather her thoughts. "There is a cache of gold and silver coins . . . actually several caches . . . buried in secret locations in the South and Southwest. I've seen two of these small stashes my uncles unearthed. One was in a teapot, and one in a glass jar. Amounted to about two thousand dollars in gold and silver coins. Rumor has it that these stores of money have been added to over the years since the war, much of it donated by raiders and outlaw bands, like Jesse James and the Youngers. The small caches are spread around and hidden according to elaborate maps and secret symbols to avoid being looted. But the story goes there is one large mother lode hidden in a remote location in New Mexico. Presently only two men know the exact location of this hoard, and one of them is my grandfather, who is head of his castle. . . ."

"Castle?"

"The term used to describe a cell of the Knights of the Golden Circle. The second man is my cousin, Darrel Weaver. A third man, Walter Clayton, patriarch of the Clayton family, knows only that the cache is somewhere in New Mexico Territory."

"I think I see where this is going. It sounds like a bunch of boys playing at secret clubs and competing for treasure."

"I'm sure it does . . . with all the knights playing dress-up in hooded capes, the secret handshakes to signify membership, the oaths, the hocus-pocus. But I can assure you, these grown men take it very seriously."

Kent leaned back in his seat with a half-mocking smile on his face. "The Knights of the Golden Circle, The Sons of Liberty, the Copperheads . . . they're all defunct. Have been for years. This is Eighteen Ninety, for God's sake!"

"Even though I've been excluded as a younger female, I know the knights borrowed a lot of their ritual from the Masons, who took it centuries ago from the Knights Templar. All this goes back a long way," she said, ignoring his derision.

Kent said nothing as he waited for her to continue.

"Getting back to the money, the purpose for collecting this hoard, which makes the stash in my bag look like small change, was to finance the establishment of a new country, consisting of a couple of Southern states, several Caribbean islands, and Mexico. At this moment, diplomats from the Knights of the Golden Circle are calling on the heads of state in Mexico, and leading politicians in South Carolina, Georgia, and Mississippi."

"We fought a war to preserve the Union," Rasmussen said. "Do they want to do it all over again? Pardon me for saying so, but you seem entirely too sensible to believe that rubbish."

"I don't. But if you lived among my people for a few months, you'd find yourself being convinced it was an attractive possibility . . . no, even a definite probability." She looked at his amused, ridiculing expression. How to make him understand? "In the space of one generation, my family went from wealthy, slave-holding planters to dirt-poor farmers and laborers."

"What about the Claytons?"

"My grandfather, Silas Newburn, is seventy-eight years old. When he was much younger, he helped encode the secret map that holds the location of the mother lode. Walter Clayton, the seventy-six-year-old patriarch of the Clayton clan, knows only the approximate location. He didn't help establish this secret stash at the beginning of the war, and surely didn't approve of stolen money being added to it over the years. I've been told that the handful of knights who hid the original treasure are dead."

She paused to collect her thoughts. "Here's the problem. Before Grandpa Silas dies, he wants to see the machinery in motion for the creation of this new nation, wants his legacy to be remembered by history as one of the founding fathers. His former friend, Walter Clayton, on the other hand, wants this treasure stash so he can enrich his own family and endow his descendents with considerable wealth."

"Has either of these old men made a move to get this cache?"

"Yes. Three years ago, Grandpa Silas secretly sent two of my uncles and a couple of cousins, including my first cousin, Darrel Weaver, to New Mexico."

"And . . . ?"

"Darrel, who's my age, made it home weeks later, wounded, and told of being ambushed in a remote cañon. The other three Newburns died. Less than a month later, Andy Clayton, a braggart and bully, was found in the woods with ten bullet holes in him. None of these murders has been solved. Local sheriff shrugs it off as part of the feud."

"So your cousin, Darrel Weaver, who survived the ambush, knows the location of the treasure?"

She nodded. "I don't know how much Grandpa

told him, or showed him on a map, but it must have been enough to find it."

"So that's at least three men still living who know the location."

"Two," she corrected him. "Grandpa and Darrel. Old man Clayton knows it's somewhere in New Mexico, but that's all he knows. I've never discussed it with Darrel. And he doesn't talk about it. He still has a slug near his spine, and hate in his heart. Never misses a chance to take a swipe at the Claytons, short of murder."

"How do you and this bag of greenbacks figure into it?" She had his full attention now.

"During the war, a lot of Confederate money was squirreled away in Canadian banks for safekeeping. . . ."

"Confederate paper money became worthless," he interrupted. "It was eventually called shinplasters."

"Confederate *gold* wasn't worthless. That's what was deposited in Windsor before the larger treasure stash was taken and hidden out West. This cash I have has been in a foreign account, drawing interest for twenty-seven years. After the knights met in formal conclave, the ruling council appointed me as the most likely person to go north, withdraw the money, and close the account. I was chosen since I had nothing to do with any of this, and wasn't born until Eighteen Sixty-Two. I would be the least suspected of anyone in the family. My cover story was that I was going to visit an elderly aunt on my mother's side in Windsor. But apparently word somehow leaked to the Claytons, and Johnny was put on my trail."

"Why did you take the money in cash, instead of a bank draft?"

"Grandpa Silas doesn't trust banks. Wanted it in gold, but that's too heavy for me to carry and would draw too much attention. It will be converted to coin later, since gold talks in international circles and the state houses."

"I see."

She hesitated before continuing. "There's another, personal, reason I was sent. I'd done something to disgrace the Newburn family name. If I successfully complete this mission, I'll be forgiven and welcomed back by all . . . except maybe a few of the backbiting women."

"Should I know what it is?"

She shook her head slowly, feeling her cheeks growing warmer. "It's a personal matter . . . irrelevant."

"Is it possible this Johnny Clayton was sent to watch and make sure you didn't abscond with the money?"

"Sent by whom? Not my family. He's a Clayton, and they want the money for themselves. I know Johnny. He wants the two hundred and fifty thousand dollars in this bag for himself."

"Do you think he'd actually harm you to get it?"

"He wouldn't hesitate to squash me like a tick," she said with more feeling than she intended.

Rasmussen looked at her curiously, but she made no further explanation. How could she tell him that handsome Johnny Clayton and she had outraged both their families eight years earlier by eloping? During their wild flight, Johnny had been shot in the knee. Ever after, he blamed this wound for ending his career as a lumberjack, the only occupation he knew. For consolation, he'd taken to drink and, later, became so abusive, she left him. With no skills and unable to support herself, she'd returned home, to the scorn of her kin.

This mission would redeem her. The Knights of the Golden Circle had even promised her an $8,000 reward when she delivered the full leather satchel into her grandfather's hands.

Chapter Three

"We're coming into Chicago," Rasmussen said, glancing out the grimy window. The setting sun was a red disk dodging between the taller brick buildings as their car rumbled and swayed over rail connections and switches. After being accustomed to the crisp air of the Canadian prairie, he grimaced at the pall of smoke from rows of mills and factories.

"I have to make a stop here," he said, reaching for his hat.

Nellie grabbed him by the arm. "What for? Our tickets are through to Saint Louis. We don't even have to change. Our Pullman will be coupled to another southbound train."

"Didn't have time to buy a gun in Detroit," he said. "You'll have to come with me. I'm not letting you, or that bag, out of my sight."

She nodded. "We have an hour and a half layover. Plenty of time."

Ten minutes later they descended to the platform, Nellie clutching her drum bag. He guided her out of the busy terminal and down the sidewalk.

Rasmussen had a general idea of the type of weapon he wanted. Following the Métis uprising five years earlier, the higher powers of the Mounted Police had seen fit to equip the force with the Colt .45 1878 Model. With its 7 1/2 inch barrel, it was a hefty, accurate sidearm, fine for long range work. But now, as a civilian, he was looking for a somewhat lighter pistol to carry.

Binkleman's Hardware was a large establishment stocking thousands of tools, implements, and hardware items, in addition to a wide variety of pistols and long guns.

Rasmussen scanned the display case and the dozens of handguns hanging on wall hooks behind the counter. It'd take more time than he had to examine even half the selection.

"Help you?" offered a balding clerk in striped shirt and bow tie, smoothing the points of his waxed mustache.

"Let me see that Merwin-Hulbert."

The clerk removed the pistol from the case and handed it over. "One of the finest weapons made," he said, "although it doesn't enjoy the reputation of Colt or Smith and Wesson."

Rasmussen nodded, turning the revolver in his hands. The clerk was not just making a sales pitch; he was telling the truth. Rasmussen had seen two different models of the Merwin-Hulbert make—the first carried by a civilian scout, and the other captured from one of Louis Riel's men at Batoche. The machining and tolerances of these guns were near perfection. The vast majority of them came nickel-plated from the factory. This one was a .38-caliber, double action with a 5 1/2 inch barrel, and polished rosewood grips. He hefted it, feeling the balance, then held it at arm's length and sighted along the top of the ribbed barrel. Pressing a catch on the left side of the frame, he released the barrel and cylinder, which slid forward and tilted to the right—the manufacturer's unique design for ejecting spent cartridges. The gun had a bird's head grip. A small triangle of steel that protruded from the butt was holed to accept a lanyard. This small wedge of steel would make a fearsome, skull-splitting club as well, he noted.

"How much?"

"Thirty-five dollars."

A fair price for a quality weapon; he need not look further. "Add a holster and box of shells to that?"

"I've got a broken in, used holster that'll fit it."

"Fine." Rasmussen handed over one of the $100 bills Nellie had paid him. Might as well get some change. He'd need some smaller denominations later. "No need to wrap it. I'll wear it." He unbuckled his belt and slid the holstered gun onto his left side so the butt pointed forward. It was concealed by his corduroy jacket. He pocketed the change and receipt from the clerk. He and Nellie left the store.

A bell *clanged* sharply as a horse-drawn trolley passed. They crossed the street, dodging the wheels of a heavy dray that ground by, iron-shod draft horses clopping hollowly on the cobblestones.

"Why'd you select that particular gun?" she asked. "You didn't shop around, or look at any of the others." She hurried to keep stride with him on the sidewalk.

"Quality, workmanship, reliability, balance. The barrel is just heavy enough to dampen the recoil, and just long enough to allow me to hit a target beyond twenty feet. And it weighs less than two pounds."

"Oh." She seemed properly awed by this surfeit of information.

Within a half block, he stepped into an alleyway to be a little less conspicuous, and loaded the .38.

"You expecting trouble?"

"I wouldn't have bought this if I weren't," he replied shortly, flipping up the loading gate. He shoved the weapon into its holster and moved on at a brisk walk. It felt good to stretch his legs.

"None of the men I've seen appears to be armed," she commented.

"Not openly." Did this woman want him to use all the means at his disposal to protect her, or not? He began to feel uneasy. Maybe she wasn't telling him the whole truth. He took this assignment seriously. Was she playing some sort of game with him? He glanced at her as they hurried toward the depot. Maybe she was averse to violence. If that were the case, she should never have accepted the job of being a courier for so much cash. This woman was smart. Surely she realized the danger. As a Mountie he'd been trained to anticipate trouble and to be ready for anything. Like as not, if one were prepared, a crisis could be averted or defused.

Dusk crept along the downtown streets, pulling the mantle of darkness around the brick and stone buildings that had sprung up since the Great Fire of 1871. Wagon and foot traffic thinned at the supper hour. He was glad they'd eaten in the dining car three hours earlier.

"Slow down!" she complained. "We still have a good half hour before train time." The drum bag banged against her skirted legs as she struggled along. She'd refused his earlier offer to carry it.

He slowed his long strides, glad she had no portmanteau to haul around. She'd left her small grip, containing extra clothes and toiletries, in the Pullman.

Although relieved to have a break from the confining train, Rasmussen was wary of cities where he felt closed in, and crowds of strangers could hide potential enemies. For several years, Indians and wild animals had been his fare. Before that, a Minnesota farm. *It's all a matter of what you're used to,* he thought. City detectives or policemen might harbor the opposite view.

The American and Canadian tribes had been subdued. He'd helped put down the half-blood Métis when they aggressively asserted their rights. He didn't agree with the Canadian government's overreaction to the Métis' grievances and to the rail workers' strike, even though, as a Mounted Policeman, he'd been forced to help suppress both. That was one reason he'd left the force. With the Indian tribes confined, he was seeing the frontier change, and it made him sad in a way he couldn't explain. As much as white society had longed for this to happen, he felt something had gone out of the country, never to return, as if the last free-roaming mountain lions had been caged.

Turning the corner, he came in sight of the big, brick depot. There were enough white criminals in this city alone to make up for any number of red warriors. But what was romantic or exciting about chasing a bunch of city hoodlums?

The Pullman porter had told them their car would be connected to the southbound train parked on the sixth track out from the platform. Rasmussen turned away from the hissing gaslights of the depot and led the way around the ends of two parked trains. Red lanterns glowed on a caboose. He walked next to the cars in the closed darkness under the train shed and tried to see the lettering that would identify their Pullman.

"Oohh!"

Rasmussen whipped around at the shrill cry in time to see Nellie stagger and fall flat on her face. A figure darted away.

"My bag!" she cried. "He stole my bag!"

Running feet pounded away into the gloom. Rasmussen yanked his pistol and sprinted after the robber, his shoes *crunching* the soft cinders alongside the train. The footsteps were pulling away; the man was amazingly fast. His murky form pounded across a wooden platform with a hollow *ka-thump! ka-thump!*— the irregular pace of a limping man. The man leapt off the other side and the sound ceased. Heedless of a possible ambush, Rasmussen gritted his teeth and dashed around a boxcar. 100 feet away, a fleeing figure was silhouetted by gaslights from the depot. Rasmussen skidded to a stop in the gravel, brought up his gun, and fired twice, as fast as he could pull the trigger. His revolver bucked and flashed flame as the blasts filled the cavernous train shed, reverberating from the brick walls and rail cars.

A yelp of pain answered and the dark figure bounded out of sight. Rasmussen moved carefully forward, unable to hear anything but his ears ringing and his own harsh breathing. The small bag lay on the ground, its leather handle and small padlock shot off by one of the bullets meant for the robber. He strained his ears, but any sounds were muffled by the *chuffing* of a locomotive accelerating out of the station some distance away. Walking carefully in his new, slick-soled shoes, he peered around a pile of freight and luggage stacked on a handcar. No one. The robber had either gone to ground somewhere close, possibly waiting in ambush, or was already beyond earshot and still running. In either case, Rasmussen broke off pursuit, and let him go. The noise of shots would bring the curious, or the authorities, and he didn't want to be there when they came.

He holstered his Merwin-Hulbert, retrieved the drum bag, and noticed it was no longer secured. He snapped the latch and threw open the flap. Bundles of greenbacks greeted his gaze. He'd never seen so much money in one place. It didn't even look real. She'd been telling the truth about what she carried. He latched the bag and tucked it under one arm. Then he quickly melted into the shadows, finding his roundabout way back to the Pullman.

"What the hell was that?" he heard a distant voice shout.

"Sounded like explosions," a closer voice answered.

"Hell, that was gunfire!" the first man yelled.

Still breathing deeply and with the acrid taste of coal smoke in the back of his throat, Rasmussen approached Nellie who was leaning against their train car.

"Get aboard before somebody shows up," he said tersely. "In a city this size . . . bound to be a cop on a beat . . . just when you don't need him." He took her arm and hurried her up the steps into their Pullman. He doubted anyone had seen the confrontation, but a conductor or trainman might have been nearby.

"Oh, thank God! You got the bag!" she said. "I heard shots."

"Mine. He got away, but dropped this. Afraid the handle's shot off." He handed her the damaged bag. "You hurt?"

"A little bruised is all."

In the light of the dimmed overhead lamps they moved along the aisle to their numbered berths, which the porter had already made up for the night. She thrust the bag inside the curtains of the lower bunk, and sat down on the edge. Rasmussen stood in the aisle, clinging to the edge of the upper berth. The damaged toes on his right foot were burning. He wondered if he'd ever get over the effects of that frostbite.

"See why I wanted you to protect me?" she said.

"That was no casual robber. That was your man with the limp . . . Johnny Clayton. I didn't see his face," he said, "but, for a man with a bad leg, he can run like an antelope."

"Johnny was always lean and quick. A good athlete. He knew what he wanted. Yanked the bag so hard, he threw me down." She rubbed her wrist. "Did you . . . shoot him?" she asked.

He noted the hesitancy in her voice. "Don't think so . . . too far off." He drew a long breath. "Got clean away. One lucky shot hit the bag. Heard him yell. Could've stung his hand. If I did clip him, it didn't slow him down."

"Oh." She seemed relieved.

They were silent for a few moments.

Other passengers filed into the car, began stowing their hand luggage and preparing to settle in for the night.

"I'll take the upper," Rasmussen said, tossing his saddlebags with their meager cargo into the top bunk. "And we probably need to find a safer place for that bag."

"I'm going to the washroom at the end of the car," she said, pushing the scuffed bag toward him. "Keep this safe till I get back."

"So you finally trust me with it?" He smiled rue-fully.

"You didn't have to bring it back to me," she reminded him, moving toward the rear of the car.

The Pullman lurched into motion and began to roll, carrying them away from danger. Or was it? A doubt clouded his mind. Johnny Clayton had eluded him, and could very well be aboard this train, wounded or not.

Chapter Four

Nellie awoke. Between slitted eyelids she saw the gray of dawn filtering through the partially curtained window beside her. She closed her eyes and snuggled down into the soft mattress. Plenty of time yet to be rocked back to sleep by the gentle swaying of the Pullman.

"Nell! Get up!"

She cringed at the sound of Rasmussen's voice just outside the curtain. "It's too early," she protested. "How far to Saint Louis?"

"We'll be crossing the Mississippi bridge in ten minutes." He pulled back the curtain and she saw he was already dressed. "We have to make our connection for Rolla and Springfield," he continued.

"Don't you think I know that? I came up on the Frisco Line."

"Yeah, but I'm having second thoughts about going back the same way."

"Why?"

"I just got my first good look at Johnny Clayton."

"What?" She sat up abruptly, bumping her head on the underside of the upper berth. "He's on this train?" She was suddenly wide awake. "Where?"

"I was in the dining car, having coffee, when he

came in. I recognized the limp. He had his left hand wrapped. I went over, sat down, and we talked."

"You did what?"

"I introduced myself and told him that as long as we were going to be enemies, we might as well get to know each other."

Nellie reflected that the male species never ceased to amaze and puzzle her. She waited for him to continue.

"He already guessed you'd hired me for protection, so I told him that, if he came near you or tried to rob us, he'd think he was tangling with a mountain lion." He smiled grimly. "Might have been a little over-dramatic."

"What did he say to that?" She knew her estranged husband would not have openly challenged the bigger, stronger Rasmussen.

"Of course he didn't admit to anything. I asked how he'd hurt his hand, and he said he'd cut it on a broken bottle." Rasmussen chuckled, keeping his voice low since many of the passengers in the car still slept. "Told him next time his injury could be worse. Complained my aim was off last night, or he might be lying in a Chicago morgue. Think I ruined his appetite 'cause he turned a bit pale and didn't eat much before he left."

"You just let him go?" She was incredulous.

"Of course. He's done nothing illegal that I can prove. I didn't even have a look at his face last night in Chicago. But he got the message, even if I did lay it on like an actor in a melodrama. Johnny Clayton didn't impress me as stupid. He'll take the message to heart and we'll hear no more of him."

"You don't know Johnny," she said. "His pride can't take insults or threats or humiliation. Most of his family's like that. That's why this damnable feud has gone on so long."

"You think he'll make another try before we get to Springfield?"

"Yes. The closer we get to home, the more desperate he'll be. He knows he won't have a chance at the money once I turn it over to Grandpa."

"We'll shake him off our trail."

"How do you propose to do that?"

"By pretending to board the Frisco, then slipping out to catch a steamboat at the riverfront."

"Can't be done." She shook her head, running the fingers of one hand through her tangled hair. "We could catch the boat, but where would that take us? If we went ashore at some landing in the boot heel, we'd have to travel overland to Springfield . . . nearly all the way across the state. The Ozark country has rocky ridges and looping streams. Heavy forest. Summer days so hot and muggy you can hardly get your breath. Plenty of ticks, chiggers, 'skeeters, and snakes. No east and west trains. A few roads wind in and out among those hill farms and villages. You don't want to go that way. Even if we bought horses, and had no accidents and tolerable weather, it'd likely take us a couple of weeks to cross Missouri. And I sure don't want to try it carrying all this cash." She didn't say so, but neither did she want to be discovered by the natives traveling in the company of a man with a Yankee accent. "Shut that curtain so I can dress," she finished. "We can discuss this over breakfast."

"Wear something a little more practical, if you have it," he said through the curtain. "Like a riding skirt and boots, maybe."

Thirty minutes later they were eating eggs and

toast in the dining car while the train sat stationary in the St. Louis station. A nervous stomach kept her from enjoying the food since she kept looking over her shoulder for the saturnine face of Johnny Clayton. It was unlikely he'd show up now, but she couldn't relax. The stagecoach bag rested under the table between her booted feet. She'd put on fresh undergarments, a white cotton blouse, and a mid-calf cotton skirt. It was her only other outfit and she felt like a cowgirl among all the other lady passengers in their fashionable summer attire. But she smiled inwardly with the personal knowledge of how hot even the lightest of those long linen and cotton dresses could be.

". . . you know this region and I don't," Rasmussen was saying. "We'll stick with the train as the most direct route and take our chances. I don't think he's likely to ambush us on a crowded train. Any other personal confrontation, I can handle. In the meantime, you and I and that bag will be like this." He held three fingers together.

"Maybe not quite that close." She smiled.

They finished eating, gathered up their few belongings, and debarked onto the platform. Rasmussen had used his spare belt to strap the damaged stagecoach bag, forming a loop for a makeshift handle. For now, he carried their precious luggage, along with his saddlebags.

The sun had risen only an hour earlier, but already the June day promised to be steamy. She breathed with relief as they entered an airy, high-ceilinged waiting room that gave the illusion of coolness. The place bore a faint aroma of coal smoke and cigars. People streamed through the massive depot, buying tickets, checking schedules and baggage at the

counters, rushing to catch trains, going for breakfast
in the restaurant. Arriving travelers dropped suit-
cases to embrace loved ones. After nine days on the
road, the sight made her homesick. She hoped this
day would pass quickly; they were due to arrive in
Springfield by eight that night. She caught herself
unconsciously scanning the flowing crowd for a
man with a limp.

Her reverie was broken when Rasmussen paused
to examine a large railroad map of Missouri mounted
on a wall. She, too, studied it, noting the rail lines
running south of St. Louis that were denoted in red
against the green map. The St. Louis-San Francisco
Line snaked southwest across the state toward
Springfield and beyond. Another branch of the same
road ran southward along the Mississippi. A third
line—the Missouri Pacific—passed through Poplar
Bluff and down into Arkansas. Lines on a map—
they looked so simple. But she knew the rough terrain they crossed, and was grateful the two of them
would not have to journey by horse and wagon.

By the time they drank cold lemonade in the station restaurant, it was time to board. They didn't
need a Pullman now; she'd reserved a parlor car for
this leg of the trip. Damn the expense. No more of
those uncomfortable day coaches with the bench
seats like she'd ridden north.

The train crawled toward the edge of the city,
then picked up speed, leaving the scattered houses
behind and plunging into the heavy hardwood forest that clothed the Ozark Plateau far south into
Arkansas.

She sat next to Rasmussen in an upholstered
high backed armchair. Anchored to the floor, the
chairs could swivel in any direction, or be tilted

backward for a nap. The open windows admitted a pleasant breeze, and now and then a puff of coal smoke. Thank heaven the locomotive's stack had spark arresters to prevent a showering of fine cinders.

For the first half hour, they hardly spoke, each engrossed in thought. Nellie had come to expect reticence from this man, who was all business. That suited her fine; she hadn't intended to hire a jovial traveling companion. She glanced over and saw he'd removed his corduroy coat, exposing the holstered pistol at his lean waist. The heat had reduced him to the very picture of a casual traveler, with no celluloid collar or tie, shirt sleeves rolled up. He leafed through a copy of *Harper's Weekly*, appearing to have difficulty keeping his eyes open.

She pulled her gaze away to stare out at the green wall of trees sliding past, nearly brushing the sides of the train. She wondered if she should tell Kent about her relationship with Johnny. Would it make any difference? Probably not. She was sure Kent would do whatever was necessary to protect her and the money. Besides, she and Johnny had parted, childless, several years ago. The fire of their romance and passion had long since burned out. She didn't know if he'd continued to drink.

For some reason he was desperate to get his hands on the cash she carried. At first she thought he wanted the money for himself. It would make him a rich man, all right, but Johnny had never been greedy during their marriage, although he was often out of work. More likely he was under family pressure. Perhaps they'd promised him something in return for capturing the money. Or threatened him if he didn't. Old man Clayton could be even harsher and more demanding than her own grandfather. Maybe the two patriarchs were carrying on their feud through their grandchildren.

A sudden break in the trees opened up a long vista. The midday sun bore down on two cultivated fields planted in tobacco and corn. A small house sat on the edge of cleared land in the distance.

The locomotive's steam whistle wailed a warning and a half minute later a crossing of a dirt road flashed past her window. She could hear the brakes grinding as the train slowed on a downgrade and rounded a long curve. Looking ahead, she saw a spindly wooden trestle. The heavy car swayed as the train crept across. She noticed Kent sitting upright and tight-lipped, eyes fixed on the smooth-flowing green river in the gorge below. She hadn't ridden many trains in her life, but knew that most rail lines had abysmal safety records. She had no fear of dying in the flaming wreckage of a rail car, any more than she feared snakebite or swamp fever. Trestles weakened by floods or neglect were just another possibility in an uncertain world, and she ignored them all with the fatalistic confidence of youth.

As the day wore on, she found herself relaxing. In spite of the likelihood that her husband was aboard this very train, she'd seen no sign of him. Every mile that rolled under the wheel trucks, every hour that unwound from her small pocket watch meant she was closer to home and safety. She never knew a small leather bag with $250,000 worth of paper currency could be so heavy. Or did it just seem that way?

The train stopped briefly at Cuba and again at

Rolla to discharge and take on passengers and mail.

The conductor strolled through their car, punching the tickets of local riders. "Lebanon, next stop!" he called, moving down the aisle. "Lebanon, Missouri, next stop in thirty minutes."

"Kent, Lebanon is only forty miles from Springfield," Nellie said, touching Rasmussen's arm to rouse him from a doze. "I should stop and wire Grandpa to meet us."

Rasmussen nodded. "Does he live in town?"

"Oh, no. He's on the old home place, ten miles south. The telegraph agent will send a boy on horseback to deliver the message." She paused. "I'm to use the code word 'done' to let him know my mission was successful."

"Does he expect you today?"

"This week was as close as I could estimate my return. Grandpa's been troubled with rheumatism of late. He might send my uncle."

"Where's your father?"

She felt a familiar twinge in her stomach at the mention of her parent.

"Gunned down from ambush six years ago. We suspect the Claytons, but nobody was ever caught or tried for it. Like I said earlier, the local sheriff hopes we'll keep killing each other off, and good riddance to all."

The train ground to a halt at 7:30, and the engineer positioned the locomotive under the spout of a water tank.

Rasmussen slipped on his corduroy jacket and slung his saddlebags over one shoulder. He took charge of the stagecoach bag and its precious cargo, while Nellie carried only her small grip with a change of clothes and personal items. They debarked onto the stone platform of a long brick depot.

"Where's the town?" he asked, glancing around at the solid banks of trees behind the station.

"When the Frisco came through here a few years back, the Lebanon town council wouldn't donate any land to build a depot, so the rail line located out here, nearly two miles from town."

"Cut off their nose to spite their face," he commented.

"Western Union is in that little building next door," she said, pointing.

Two porters in stiff-brimmed caps passed them, pushing a baggage cart piled high with boxes and mail sacks. The big iron wheels of the handcart turned in front of them, blocking their way. Rasmussen stepped aside to go around. The two porters were suddenly on him, one pinning his arms and the other snatching the Merwin-Hulbert from its holster and shoving the muzzle into Rasmussen's chest.

Nellie started to scream, but a dirty, callused hand clamped over her mouth from behind while a fourth man clubbed Kent with the barrel of a pistol. He slumped forward, stunned. She twisted and struggled to no avail as the two porters and another man dressed as a railroad worker in overalls and brogans dragged her and Kent behind the depot into the woods. She rolled her eyes and looked about frantically for help, but apparently no one had seen or heard the quick, silent assault in the late afternoon shadows behind the loaded luggage cart. The view of the Western Union office had also been effectively blocked. The few men she glimpsed passing in and out of the depot were on business of their own, and didn't look in her direction.

The three men forced their two captives more than fifty yards into the woods before they stopped.

"I'll take my hand away if you don't scream," a whiskey voice said in her ear.

Her lungs heaving and nostrils flaring, she nodded. The hand was removed, and she gasped gratefully. Her captor kept her arms pinned from behind.

Rasmussen was recovering his senses, looking around.

A lean porter shoved a pistol into his chest. "Make a sound and I'll kill you."

Rasmussen said nothing. A small spot of blood soaked through his thick blond hair near the crown of his head.

"Hurry. Get that rope," barked one of the men.

A red-faced man in overalls slipped out of a coil of rope he'd been wearing across his barrel chest like a bandoleer.

In less than a minute Rasmussen and Nellie were pushed to the ground on either side of an elm tree, and faced the two-foot-thick trunk with their arms and legs embracing it. The rope was looped around both of them and the tree, the knots tightly secured. Nellie didn't trust herself to speak for fear she would break into sobs. She knew—they all knew—what this was about. The quarter million in cash. One of the porters emptied Rasmussen's saddlebags onto the ground and the other porter proceeded to stuff the bundles of greenbacks into it, apparently for easier transport.

"Nice-looking gun," a big, mustachioed man said, examining Rasmussen's nickel-plated Merwin-Hulbert. "But I can't figure out how to open the damned thing. Reckon I can get a few bucks for it, though."

"No you won't. That gun is too distinctive. It could tie us to this robbery," came from behind Nellie.

She jerked her head around as far as she could from her cramped position. That voice was all too familiar. Johnny Clayton was standing there, his hand swathed in a white bandage.

"What do ya mean . . . tie us to this robbery?" The big man snorted. "They can see our faces, can't they?"

"It's our word against theirs, if it ever comes to that," Clayton said. "The gun would be physical evidence we were here. Leave it!"

The mustachioed man tossed the weapon on the ground with the empty stagecoach bag and Nellie's small grip.

Two short blasts on the steam whistle announced the train's imminent departure.

"Let's go, boys," Clayton said, staring at Nellie. "It wouldn't do to miss our ride."

He'd slipped off the train to rendezvous with his men in the woods, she decided. All very neatly planned.

Johnny's lean, dark face was not smiling. "Sorry, Nell," he said, sounding as if he really meant it. "I had to do it. We won't gag you, but you'll holler a long time before anyone hears you back here." He had the worn, hollow-eyed appearance of someone who'd been drinking a lot more than he'd been eating or sleeping.

Then the four men were running through the sparse undergrowth toward the depot, the loaded saddlebags bouncing on Clayton's shoulder.

"Damn you, Johnny!" she shrieked. "You can't leave us here!"

Chapter Five

Embarrassed, more than hurt, Rasmussen leaned his forehead against the rough bark, thankful the thick bole of the elm screened his face from Nellie. Here he sat, hugging a tree, bound hand and foot, the woman he'd sworn to protect sitting opposite him in the same predicament. Worst of all, the $250,000 he had been guarding was missing, swiped so skillfully there'd been very little violence and no noise. He hadn't even had a chance to put up a fight.

"You hurt bad?" Nellie asked from the opposite side of the tree.

"No."

"Quit trying to sound tough," she said. "I saw your head bleeding."

"Scalp wounds bleed a lot. Just a dull ache now. No dizziness. I'll be OK."

The blow to his pride had been worse. Somehow it helped to talk. Relief at escaping alive had made him almost giddy. Or was it the blow to the head? He was glad he hadn't been struck with the butt of his Merwin-Hulbert with its skull-splitting wedge of steel. The men had worn no masks and could be identified later. He'd never dealt with criminals like this. It was far different from tracking and arresting Americans who crossed into Canada to sell whiskey to the Indians.

Sometimes the Mounties had encountered armed resistance when the whiskey peddlers were cornered, but as a policeman he was always on the offensive, not the defensive. This time, he was the hunted, not the hunter, and he'd not been up to the challenge. It was unclear to him why the robbers had left two live witnesses. Extreme confidence of the professional, or extreme stupidity of the amateur, were his only guesses. Perhaps they operated on some Southern code of honor that stopped short of murder—a hanging offense.

"What's next?" she asked. "This rope is cutting off circulation in my wrists."

"Get loose and send a telegram to your grandfather."

The huffing of the locomotive faded as the train pulled away. The peaceful sounds of Nature settled around them—the scuffing of a squirrel in the dry leaves, the trilling of a nearby mockingbird.

"We could strain back against the loops and then let up to see if we can stretch it a little," she suggested.

"This new hemp won't give enough to matter. And it would just pull the knots tighter." He thought for a few moments. Their hands were overlapping. "I can reach the knots on your wrists," he said. "Move your left hand up a little." He began patiently to work the hard knot, nails trying to get a grip and tug it open. It was discouraging work. "This might take a while," he said. "Just relax." He didn't want to tell her it might be impossible.

"Hard to relax in this position."

They fell silent as he continued to struggle, his

strong fingers plucking, getting purchase, twisting, tugging. Perspiration began to trickle down his face in the still, humid atmosphere.

"Something's biting me on the legs," she said, squirming. "Could be flies, or ants, or beetles, or anything!"

Rasmussen ignored her anguished imagination. He had troubles of his own, breathing deeply with the concentrated strain. He managed to wedge a finger under one of the tiny loops and began to work it loose. It took another ten minutes, but he pulled it partially free. Leaning hard to the right, he could barely see his right hand; he operated mostly by touch. He swore softly as he bent back a fingernail against the stubborn knot. But he kept at it, doggedly. "Ahh . . . there she goes!" The knot relaxed its grip, and Nellie pulled the loops free from her left hand.

From there it was only a matter of minutes for her to free herself, and then Rasmussen. They got up, brushed themselves off, and stretched their stiff limbs. The boots had protected Nellie's ankles, but she rubbed her chafed wrists.

Rasmussen retrieved his pistol from the ground, checked its loads and action, and blew a few specks of dirt from it. Good as new. He holstered it, then stuffed his few belongings into the empty stagecoach bag, and handed Nellie her own small grip.

"We have one less bag to carry," she remarked without emotion, as if still in shock.

"You feeling OK?" he asked.

"Yeah." She nodded without looking at him.

"Let's go." He led the way out of the shaded woods toward the Western Union office, Nellie hurrying to keep up.

But there was no need to rush.

"Line's been dead for two hours," the telegrapher told them when they asked to send a wire to Springfield. "Don't know when it'll be operating again. Likely a tree limb down on the wire somewhere."

They conferred outside on the platform. "Might've known they'd cut the wire first thing. Is there any way we can rent a couple horses or a rig and beat the train to Springfield?" Rasmussen asked.

"Not from here. The road's decent, but the train clips right along. It'll be there in less than an hour."

Rasmussen nodded. "Does the train make any more stops?"

"No. Not even for water."

"Then they aren't likely to jump off somewhere before they reach Springfield. Too much risk of injury . . . or drawing attention to themselves from other passengers."

They checked with the depot ticket agent and learned the next westbound train wasn't scheduled until the next afternoon. The hack that transported passengers to and from town had already left, so they walked the two miles into Lebanon.

They were mostly silent on the hike. But, as they approached town, Rasmussen said: "I don't suppose it would do any good to say I'm sorry."

"Won't change anything, if that's what you mean," Nellie replied, looking at her boot toes scuffing along in the road dust. "We're both in a fix. I failed in the mission I was given. So, not only will all those busybodies start a whispering campaign that I let the Claytons steal it on purpose, but. . . ."

"Why would they do that?" Rasmussen interrupted.

"I neglected to tell you that Johnny Clayton and I were married for a few years."

He looked up, surprised. "Nice time to tell me."

"Would it have made any difference?"

"Probably not," he replied slowly. "But I might have treated him differently when we met in the dining car. Maybe would have put him off the train, or taken some other precaution."

"I doubt it," Nellie said. "You men are all alike. You thought you had him bluffed out. I'm sure he wired ahead and arranged to have those men waiting for us at the Lebanon depot. I recognized that fat one with the mustache as one of his cousins."

Rasmussen stopped in the deserted road and turned to face her. "Before today this Johnny Clayton was only a nuisance, not to be taken seriously. Now I'm going after him with everything I've got."

"For the sake of the money, or your hurt pride?" she asked.

"Both. You hired me to do a job, and I failed. The man simply humiliated me without even exerting himself. And got away with a quarter million dollars. I'm not letting him get away with that."

"What's your plan?"

"Too late to mount a chase today. We'll get a hotel tonight, then either catch tomorrow's train to Springfield, or hire a rig or saddle horses."

"Doubt if the Claytons will be hard to find," she said. "Probably won't see Johnny or those other men, but word about them having the money will circulate like it was only a rumor. They'll make both of us the butt of their jokes while they're bustin' their buttons with pride." She shook her head. "You won't find any evidence. Unfortunately I know how they operate. I'll catch hell from both Grandpa Newburn and from the Claytons."

"I'll tell your grandfather what happened, and take the blame."

"No. He'll believe my story, all right. I've never lied to him. And all the responsibility is on my shoulders. I should've taken a bank draft for that money, in spite of what the old man wanted. But that's all water through the millrace. It's gone and I won't receive the eight thousand I was promised for completing the job, and you won't get paid, either."

He reached for his billfold and extracted four $100 bills. "Here's most of what's left."

"Keep it. You earned it. Except for your quick action, I'd have lost that money in Chicago."

"Lost is lost."

She waved off the money and started walking again. "I've got enough to see me home. That's all I need."

"Why go back?" he asked. "Find some place where you're not known and settle down."

"I'd be suspected of taking the money, myself, or conspiring with Johnny to take it. Besides, I couldn't support myself. I have no honest skills anyone wants. I hear there are lots of prostitutes out West," she added thoughtfully.

He was startled she'd even consider the world's oldest profession, much less mention it aloud. But then she came from a rough environment, even though she said her family had been wealthy and educated before the war, at least by backwoods standards.

"There's the Gasconade Hotel," she said, pointing toward a long, two-story frame building, featuring a slanting, second empire-style roof with dormer windows.

"Looks new."

"Only a couple years old. Built mainly to house all the people the town expected to come and bathe in the magnetic water. But the crowds haven't shown up here like they do down in Hot Springs, Arkansas."

"What magnetic water?"

She gave a dismissive wave, as if she didn't want to go into a long explanation. "Workers digging a town well two years ago noticed their metal tools attracting nails. The tools had taken on magnetic properties after immersion in this water." She made a long-suffering face at him. "Of course, the town fathers just naturally figured the water had some kind of special healing powers, so they built a building over the well and tried to sell the stuff to the public as a cure-all."

"Ever try it yourself?" he asked with a grin as they approached the hotel.

"Nothing wrong with me I need to have cured," she replied.

"Not even a wart or a wrinkle?" he persisted.

She paused at the door of the hotel and looked at him. "I think that knock on the head must have addled your brains."

"Just trying to lighten the mood a little." He sighed. "Maybe take my mind off what just happened."

"I'm trying to work up my courage and figure what I'm going to say when I get home," she said. "Like as not, the news will be spread before I get there." She paused. "Maybe I can elicit a little sympathy if I pretend I was roughed up and hurt."

"You don't strike me as the lying type."

"Lying isn't one of my faults," she admitted.

"I'll tell them it was all my fault for failing to do my job. Nobody could blame you for what happened."

"My grandpa expects results, not excuses."

"You make him sound like a real ogre."

"Strict, unbending, stubborn describe him better. He's not malicious."

Rasmussen shook his head. "For the life of me, I can't imagine why you want to go back."

She shrugged. "Family ties. Everyone has problems. Nothing's solved by running away from them." She looked up at him. "Even you probably have a few things you'd rather not face."

He thought of his own departure from the Mounted Police. Never had he considered it running away—until now. This petite brunette was beginning to get into his head. He'd been put off by her at first, but, in the few days they'd known each other, he'd grown to like and respect her. Artifice was not in her nature.

She took the small grip from his hand and opened the hotel door. "I'll be all right from here." She hesitated. "You know, I'm in no hurry to get home, so I won't take tomorrow's train. Let's rent horses at the livery and ride the rest of the way. Give Grandpa time to cool off . . . possibly even get a little worried about me. If he hears I was robbed and then don't show up, he might start a full-scale war with the Claytons by the time I get there."

They spent the night in adjacent rooms and even took time, next morning, to bathe in tin bathtubs of magnetic water in the health spa on the ground floor. The water seemed no different to him than any other. Perhaps that was the reason the hotel appeared nearly empty. Rasmussen soaked the dried blood from his hair and washed the tender gash that already was beginning to heal. Then he shaved and put on his only clean shirt before meeting Nellie in the dining room for breakfast. It was almost as if they were enjoying a holiday outing.

By ten o'clock they'd had a lunch packed by the hotel, rented two saddle horses at the local livery, and were on their way.

The dirt road, rutted and dusty, was not overgrown between the wheel tracks—apparently a frequently used thoroughfare. They rode in the shade of maples, oaks, elms, locusts, all competing for space in the sun. Sunlight filtered green through the dense hardwood forest, not penetrating the overhead canopy. The activities of settlement and the axe had left no mark here, Rasmussen thought. Beautiful as it was, he couldn't help but think how easily an ambush could be laid in these woods. He said little as they rode along, not finding it necessary to keep up a conversation.

Now and then Nellie pointed at an armadillo waddling off the road, or the pointed nose and ears of a red fox watching them intently from a clearing. Her eyes were accustomed to picking out things in the woods.

The road dipped and rose, sometimes following a ridge line, then gradually winding down into a valley to ford a pebbly stream.

"There's a hellbender salamander!" she cried, pointing.

At first Rasmussen couldn't distinguish the motionless gray-brown lizard from its background of dirt and leaves. Then he saw the beady eyes in the flat head. Loose, wrinkled skin seemed too large for its body. For several seconds, the foot-long reptile regarded their approach, then skittered away, disappearing under a weedy cutbank.

"Ugly cuss," Rasmussen remarked. "Looks like he's wearing hand-me-downs."

She grinned. "They're harmless. So homely, they're cute. Far as I know, they're found only in the Ozarks."

They rode up out of the stream, the horses' hoofs clattering on a ledge of bare rock.

"Good shady place to stop for lunch," he suggested, his stomach growling.

They dismounted, putting the horses on long leads to graze or water, then spread out a blanket and sat down to eat their sandwiches and drink their jugs of lemonade.

Rasmussen salted a tomato. This was as quiet and peaceful a place as he'd ever been. Chewing thoughtfully, he tuned his senses to the surrounding Nature—the *hum* of bees probing for nectar in the orange flowers of trumpet vines; the soft gurgling of water over smooth stones in the streambed; the rustling of overhead cottonwood leaves that scattered spots of noonday sun across the pale sandstone; the varied trills of mockingbirds in the trees.

He savored the moment. Regardless of the strains and pain of the past, or the dangers and turmoil of an unknown future, here was temporary respite. Without such placid intervals, he thought, humans couldn't survive the rest.

Nellie, who sat a few feet away, legs tucked beside her, seemed comfortable in his company. They had a lot to learn about each other, but every hour he spent with her seemed to increase his attraction to her. This was a natural reaction to having endured a lot together in their short acquaintance.

A half hour later they packed up their saddlebags, remounted, and moved on.

The sun was declining behind a hill when Nellie drew rein in an open glade and dismounted rather stiffly. "My bottom isn't used to the saddle," she groaned.

Rasmussen smiled. Not a lady-like comment, but honest. He swung down and stood beside her, holding his horse's reins. The shadows lengthened. Dusk crept into these coves and hollows earlier than on the vast open prairies he'd known.

Even though he'd agreed to ride part way with her, neither had mentioned anything about him turning back. Maybe this was the time. If his estimate was correct, they couldn't be over a dozen miles from Springfield. From here on, she'd be in familiar territory. She mounted again. He followed, wondering how far he should go. If she intended to reach town, she'd have to finish sometime after dark. And he wasn't about to abandon her to ride it alone.

Five minutes later, the dilemma was solved. As their tired horses walked around a bend in the road, a man in overalls and straw hat stepped from the brush, holding a double-barreled shotgun.

"Hold it right there!" he barked. "Light down offen them nags."

Chapter Six

They dismounted as ordered. The man stepped toward them, lowering the shotgun from shoulder to waist level. In the dusk under the trees, Rasmussen could see few details of the lean figure, except the faded overalls. A short, white beard was visible beneath the tattered straw hat brim.

The man peered closely at Rasmussen, then turned his attention on the woman.

"You. . . ."

"Aren't. . . ."

Each blurted out simultaneously, then stopped.

"Uncle Billy?" Nellie ventured.

"You're that Newburn girl . . . Nellie, ain't it?" he answered.

"Yes." Her voice told her relief.

"Well, I'm a suck-egg mule. What're you doin' prowlin' around here?"

"Why are you robbing strangers on the road to Springfield?"

"You ain't on the road to Springfield. You must 'a' taken the left fork a mile back, 'cause this track goes to my place."

Nellie looked confused. "I guess I did. The road didn't have a sign and I just guessed."

"You're a few miles from the Newburn place. And it's comin' on nightfall." He kept the shotgun in the crook of his arm as he turned to Rasmussen. "This one o' your'n?"

"No kin. Just a friend to keep me safe on the road."

"Safe, is it?" the wiry man chortled. "If an old geezer like me can get the drop on him that easy, he'd best take up another line o' work."

"Kent Rasmussen, this here's Uncle Billy," Nellie said.

"Pleased to meet a relative of Nell's." He thrust out his hand, which the old man ignored.

"Hell, I ain't no kin o' hers. No offense, Nell." He nodded. "I just been known as Uncle Billy for years by a passel o' nephews and nieces."

"No last name?"

"None that I'm givin' out for free." He chuckled deep in his throat. "Besides, I'm askin' the questions here. Where're you two headed?"

"It's a long story, but I'm on my way home," Nellie said.

"Tonight?"

"Yeah."

"Where'd you start from today?"

"Lebanon."

"To the Newburn place from here is six miles o' woods, cross country, and at least a dozen miles by road to Springfield and on down thataway." He stepped to one side and eyed the drooping heads of their mounts. " 'Tain't none o' my affair, and you can go on if you like, but your animals look plumb tuckered. And I'd guess you ain't et yet. You're both welcome to stay the night at my place."

Nellie looked at Rasmussen, and he nodded.

"Thanks. We'd take that kindly," she replied. "I'm kinda turned around. How far's your cabin from here?"

He jabbed the gun barrel to his right. "Only a quarter mile up to the head o' the holler." He turned and led the way. "You've stopped by here before, ain't you?"

"Once," Nellie said.

"Then you know it ain't no luxury hotel. But I reckon it beats ridin' a good long way in the dark on tired and hungry horses."

Darkness was settling in quickly. Rasmussen kept the bobbing straw hat in sight a few yards ahead as they ascended the unseen path through the undergrowth. He felt uneasy about this old man—possibly due to their experience of the day before. Or could it have been the aura of their surroundings, the oncoming night in unknown country, and the locusts screeching monotonous, undulating cadences in the trees? Then there was the sudden, silent appearance of this armed man with the singular cognomen. Rasmussen was reminded of a childhood story about gremlins materializing from the mists of an Irish bog to perform magic and mischief on unwary travelers.

Presently they came to a board shack facing down the sloping hollow toward a small branch creek. With heavy timber all about, Rasmussen was half expecting a snug log cabin, but this place had only rough planks of differing widths, probably ripped out of several logs by the local mill. At least there were screens on the door and windows, he noted while loosening the cinches on their saddles. They tied their mounts to nearby trees, and followed Uncle Billy inside.

The old man set his shotgun in a corner, flung off his straw hat, and struck a match to a coal-oil lamp on the table, turning up the wick. The soft, yellow glow revealed a neat, two-room place, everything in order and obviously the habitat of a single male. In the main room, an iron stove sat in front of a table with four straight chairs. A worn plank cupboard stood off to the left. To the right, hung a small shelf holding books and supplies. Through a partially open door, Rasmussen saw one end of a bunk.

The old hermit stirred up the coals in his stove and slid a pot of hominy and fatback onto the stove lid to reheat. "You can put your hosses in the barn out back," he said over his shoulder. "Throw some grain in that feedbox for 'em."

"Thanks." Rasmussen banged out the screen door to unsaddle and rub down the rented horses.

"Grab a couple plates and some tools there," Uncle Billy said to Nellie as Rasmussen reëntered the shack. "There's a bucket o' water by the front door if you want to wash up."

A few minutes later as the two of them sat down to eat, Uncle Billy packed a short briar pipe, stuffing the tobacco into the caked bowl with a calloused thumb. He struck a match to it and fragrant smoke swirled around him and drifted out the screen door as he leaned against the frame, arms folded. "Kinda slim fare," he said. "But I'm outta cornmeal and potatoes, and I didn't catch any perch at the crick today."

In spite of this man affecting a backwoods dialect, Rasmussen caught inflections and words that sounded inconsistent. The word "crick" was Midwestern. Nellie, a native, had used the terms "branch" and "creek". And she would've referred to this deep, grassy valley below the hills as a "cove", rather than a "hollow". Uncle Billy had called the knives and forks "tools". Rasmussen glanced at Nellie over the lip of his tin coffee cup, wishing he could have a private word with her about this man. He'd bet this hermit was as much an outlander as himself.

"You been to town or heard anything from my family the past few days?" she asked.

"No. But I gotta lay in some supplies. If you don't mind, I'll saddle the mule and ride with you tomorrow to your place afore I go on to Springfield."

This was welcome news to Rasmussen, who wasn't at all sure Nellie knew her way.

"You're going to hear this in town anyway, so I might as well tell you the straight of it," Nellie said.

"What's that?" Uncle Billy tamped down the coals in his pipe with the head of a nail.

"We were robbed at Lebanon by Johnny Clayton and three of his men."

Uncle Billy's gray eyebrows arched in surprise. "Your husband?"

"Yeah." She went on to detail what had happened.

The old man listened in silence while Rasmussen finished his meager meal.

"I'd heard rumors that you were going after a lot of money," Uncle Billy said.

"If the Claytons found out why I went to Canada, then 'most everybody knew." She nodded. "It was to bring back two hundred and fifty thousand dollars in greenbacks."

"Kind of a crazy thing to do, totin' all that cash," Uncle Billy remarked.

"That's what I thought, and you see what it came to. But tryin' to convince Grandpa is like talkin' to a stump." She shrugged. "I'm only the messenger, but I'll get the blame for it, anyway."

Uncle Billy nodded gravely, and puffed on his pipe. "Seems to me maybe your granddad likes a good fight. You ever consider that maybe the old man hung you out to dry?"

"What?" She set down her cup.

"That you were bait he was waving around to see if the Claytons would make a grab for the money?"

"Why would he do that?"

Uncle Billy shrugged and puffed on his pipe. "So he'd have an excuse to knock off a few more o' that clan? I don't know. Just a thought. I've a hunch it's a personal grudge between the heads of the families. Not so much about the money any more. More of a bare knuckle brawl to the finish between those two old roosters."

"How do you know so much about this feud?" she said. "You just came to the Ozarks last year."

"True," he said, moving to the stove and lifting the coffee pot. He refilled her cup, then Rasmussen's. "But I'm a fast learner. Whether you know it or not, I'd got wind of this Rebel treasure that'd been stashed here, there, and yon, and come here to see if I could latch onto some of it myself."

"I don't have any more use for treasure hunters than I do bounty hunters," she said.

Rasmussen didn't want to break into something that didn't concern him, but hoped she would tone down her sharp retorts. After all, they were accepting this man's hospitality. There was a time and place for everything.

But the man she called Uncle Billy didn't seem to mind. In fact, he appeared to be enjoying this repartée.

"While the Newburns and the Claytons are ripping each other apart over the big money," the old hermit said, "I'm gathering up all the loose change that falls from the table." A grin stretched his short, white beard.

"You can search till you drop dead of old age, and you won't find anything," Nellie snapped, scooping up the last spoonful of hominy.

"Oh, but I already have," Uncle Billy said around the pipe stem, hooking his thumbs into the bib of his overalls and rocking back and forth.

"I suppose we'll have to take your word on that," she remarked.

"Not at all. But the proof will have to wait until after breakfast tomorrow. I'm too tired to fool with it now."

Rasmussen continued to eat, ignoring the garrulous old man. Actually the warm food not only relieved his hunger, but was gradually making him sleepy. It was only just now full dark, probably not much later than half past nine, yet he could hardly keep his eyes open.

They chatted about the weather as the old man cleared away their dishes and washed them in water piped into the sink from a hillside spring above the shack. Nellie inquired if there was any big news about her family since she'd been gone.

"I ain't heard nothing," Uncle Billy said. "But, then, I'm up here by myself and don't hear 'less I go to town."

The old man scrounged around in a steamer trunk and produced two spare blankets for them to sleep on, then stripped to the bottoms of his long underwear and crawled into his bunk against the wall.

Rasmussen blew out the lamp and rolled into his

blanket on the wooden floor, a few feet from Nellie. To him, the solid boards felt like goose down.

"I promised to prove I've found some of the Confederate stash," Uncle Billy said next morning as they were finishing their black coffee and hard bread. "Before I show you, I'll have to collect your weapons." He reached for a percussion pistol hanging by its trigger guard over the doorway. "Not that I don't trust you, but. . . ." He held the long Remington as he removed Rasmussen's Merwin-Hulbert, then patted him for any hidden weapons. Then he did the same with Nellie, not hesitating to touch her in places Rasmussen would not have dared put his hands. She didn't object, but seemed surprised when he extracted the small pistol from her reticule. Perhaps she'd forgotten she had it.

Uncle Billy placed the two handguns on the floor next to a homemade wooden box, the size of a Wells Fargo chest. Extracting a key from a cord around his neck, he unlocked a shiny padlock and threw open the hasp. Lifting the lid, he pulled out a rawhide sack and tossed it to Rasmussen. The heavy bag *clunked* into his lap.

Rasmussen grinned. The old man had a flair for the dramatic. Opening the drawstring, he emptied the contents onto the table. The gold coins glowed in the lamplight. A few silver cartwheels peeked out from the heap.

"Nice little stash, for a start, don't you think?" The hermit had dropped his backwoods dialect and his speech had taken on a hint of culture.

"Where'd you find it?" Rasmussen heard himself asking.

"Where the Johnny Rebs hid it," the old man

replied with a chuckle. "And I'm tracking down a couple more sites that look promising."

Rasmussen and Nellie silently pawed apart the pile, spreading out the coins. Glancing at the dates, the former Mountie saw they ranged from 1850 to 1880.

"Too bad old Jesse James got put out of business so soon. He and his boys could've contributed even more to the hoard for the lost Southern cause."

Rasmussen looked at this old hermit—or whatever he was—with new respect.

"I did a lot of research before I come here," Uncle Billy continued. "So far, it's paid off. With a few more of those," he said, gesturing at the pile, "I won't have to grub for a living in my old age."

"This isn't your land," Nellie said, dully gazing at the heap on the table.

"First of all, young lady, you have no idea where I found it. Secondly, as far as I'm concerned, it's finders, keepers. That's why I'm so careful about who comes up the trail to this shack." He approached the table, gun in hand. "Probably a good idea to get me a guard dog," he added as if talking to himself. "Like y'all found out with the money you were carryin', it's better safe than sorry."

"Why are you telling us this?" Nellie asked. "Up till now, you've been a good neighbor."

"I'm still a good neighbor," he said, flipping a straight chair around and straddling it, forearms resting on the back, pistol held loosely. "But I'm a straight up sort o' fella and don't fly no false colors. If any of your kin, or the Claytons, want to keep me from snatching these small caches, let 'em try. I enjoy a challenge, a game of hide-and-seek. Adds a little pepper sauce to an old man's dull life."

Rasmussen cast a glance at him. There was more to this scruffy hermit than met the eye.

"These small stashes are scattered roundabout. They're not so easy to locate as you might think. That's the first I've found, buried in a rusty tea kettle."

"Do you have some kind of map?" Nellie asked.

"No. No inside information like that. On our way to your place, I'll show you the carvings on the rocks and trees that folks assume Indians or early Spaniards made. I can interpret most of the symbols, then apply a little logic, a compass, maybe sketch out the area on paper, use a magnet. . . . Well, I can't give away all my secrets. It's not buried deep. Found that two feet down."

Uncle Billy scooped the coins back into the sack and returned them to the chest. "Don't get no ideas about robbin' me," he said, handing back their weapons. "Maybe I don't look like much, but I'm still pretty quick on the trigger, and . . ."—he jabbed two fingers toward his face—"I'm as gimlet-eyed as a barn owl." He gave a shrill cackle that sent a shiver up Rasmussen's back.

"There isn't enough in that sack to bother about, even if we were inclined to robbery," Rasmussen scoffed, becoming irritated at the old man's antics.

"Close to six hundred dollars in there," Uncle Billy said defensively.

Rasmussen shrugged and turned his back.

Ten minutes later they were saddling up.

"Keep an eye on that crazy old man," Rasmussen said under his breath while he finished tightening the girth and dropped the stirrup into place. "No telling what he might do."

"Humor him. He's harmless," Nellie muttered without looking at him.

"You can never be too careful when dealing with crazy people."

"Eccentric, not crazy," she said softly, putting her foot in the stirrup and mounting.

"Follow me," the hermit said, kicking his mule and starting away through the trees, upslope toward the ridge top.

There was no obvious trail. But, as they surmounted the wooded summit, they emerged onto a path marked with many deer tracks. They followed this for a mile before Uncle Billy plunged off downhill through the sparse undergrowth. Except for the slanting rays of early sun bejeweling dewdrops on the bushes, Rasmussen would have had no idea of his directions.

They reached the valley floor and crossed a small creek, encountered a wagon road, and turned onto it, pointing southwest.

"Hell! If I can find my way outta here, I'll take your horse back to the Lebanon livery when I leave," Rasmussen said to Nellie as she urged her mount alongside.

"You can follow the regular road from Springfield," she replied. "This is a short cut of some kind."

Uncle Billy pulled his mule to the left of the wagon track and rode 200 yards into the dense brush where the trees were somewhat thinner. Finally, in a nearly dry, rocky streambed, he reined up and dismounted.

"Told you I'd show you where I found that stash of coins." He led his mule over the trickle of water and stopped at a boulder. "Here're some o' the markin's," he said, pointing.

Kent and Nellie dismounted. Plainly visible on the chair-size boulder were crudely incised figures of a mule or a horse, along with what appeared to be a sinuous snake.

"Hell, any kids playing in this creek could have carved those," Rasmussen said.

"But they didn't," Uncle Billy said, leading his mule a few yards along the bank. "That snake figure coincides with the curves in this crick." The old man paused and indicated more carvings—this time in the bark of a beech tree. The pictographs were not recent; the edges of the knife scars were curling inward as the tree continued trying to heal itself.

Rasmussen ran his hands over the carvings of a turtle, apparently in the process of laying eggs. The date *May 2, 1868* was inscribed, along with a carving of a palm tree and a crescent moon—pictures that meant nothing at all to him. To the height of a man on horseback, various squiggles disfigured the bark.

"Idle doodling by some would-be artist," Rasmussen said.

"The Confederates used palm trees and snakes and turtles as coding symbols. I reckon May Second, Eighteen Sixty-Eight was when the turtle laid the eggs, that is, when the coins were buried," Uncle Billy said, ignoring his comment. "Just a bit farther along here, my compass give me a signal and I found this," he said, scraping the loose ground away with his brogan. Several inches down appeared a rusted rifle barrel without a stock. "Pointed me right at it," he almost crowed, moving on up the creek about forty yards to indicate a depression in the bank that had recently been dug. "That's where my magnetic compass told me metal was buried. Found that teapot full o' coins."

"Probably the life savings of some mountaineer who didn't trust banks," Rasmussen said. "Died before he could retrieve it." In spite of himself, he was having some private doubts. Had the crazy old hermit stumbled onto one of the small caches scattered around in these hills that were actually hidden by the Knights of the Golden Circle during and after the war? Nellie had told him one or two had already been discovered.

A nice hobby for a crazy old man with nothing better to do, Rasmussen thought. But the real prize was the huge cache Nellie had said was hidden somewhere out West.

They mounted and Uncle Billy guided them back to the road, where they continued on a southwestward course. Rasmussen watched Nellie's face, trying to catch her eye to say something. But she had let her horse drop back, and her blank stare gave no clue to her thoughts. Was her mind on what they'd just seen, or on the reception that awaited her up ahead? He looped his reins over the saddle horn and used both hands to open his revolver and check the loads.

Chapter Seven

Silas Newburn paused in the front hallway to check his appearance in the tall mirror—a daily practice begun years before. His still-unlined forehead and lean cheeks were topped by a full head of neatly brushed white hair. The spade beard effectively disguised the dewlap and turkey neck beneath. He frowned at his reflection, black eyebrows drawing together. He turned sideways and sucked in his slight paunch. "Not too bad for seventy-eight," he muttered to himself, noting he was still spare and erect.

Having nothing urgent to do this morning, he'd risen later than usual and dressed informally in whipcord breeches, white shirt, brown string tie, and brown leather vest. Many of his own family thought him too formal and somewhat stuffy, but he'd acquired the habit of dressing well as a young man. Regardless of his losses of fortune during the war, he saw no reason to sink to the social level of the trashy Clayton clan.

He grunted with satisfaction and strode out onto the wide front porch, sank into a cane-bottomed rocker, tilted back, and braced his feet against the porch railing. Humid, hazy heat was already blanketing the hills and woods. But it wasn't the weather that was on his mind this morning. He was worried about his granddaughter, Nell. Nellie, as he'd always thought of her—only child of his dead son Brandon— was due home any time from the perilous mission he'd sent her on. As leader of his castle, he'd pressed his fellow knights into giving Nellie the job of being a courier for a quarter million dollars in cash—more to allow her a chance to redeem herself, than anything else. In retrospect, it seemed a foolish thing to do—and he prided himself on not doing foolish things.

No word had come from Nellie. Of course she had no way of contacting him, except perhaps by telegraph. But he knew how long the trip should take, and she was at least three days beyond her estimated arrival time—not tardy enough for great concern yet. He stared down the rutted road to where it disappeared into the woods, and felt slightly queasy. Maybe it was the breakfast of black coffee and brown bread with jam he'd fixed for himself. He didn't have much appetite as he grew older. True, food had never been his weakness. Cigars were. Eschewing an excess of the first and indulging in too many of the second had kept his body lean, but he noted with some alarm that he was becoming slightly short of breath on exertion. Mortality was staring him in the face. Time—or lack of it—was his enemy. His beloved wife of forty years had gone on ahead of him thirteen years ago. He had no fear of death himself, and seldom speculated about "that undiscovered country from whose bourne no traveler returns." He smiled at the quote from *Hamlet* that jumped into his mind. Not one of the ignorant, money-grubbing Claytons would have thought of that.

Although they respected and feared him, his own children and grandchildren looked upon him as an irascible old man who was set in his ways and had outlived his time. The men and women of his generation—his contemporaries—were mostly gone, dead of old age, illness, accidents, and violence.

But he had one more thing to accomplish before he bowed off the stage. And that was to recover the cold cache of more than $3,000,000, add it to the $250,000 in currency Nellie was bringing, and proceed quickly to establish his new republic. He, along with the treasure of many loyal Confederates, would accomplish what the terrible war had failed to accomplish—the creation of a separate, sovereign country. Very few men left any tracks of their passing on this earth. This living legacy would ensure his reputation outlived the man. He could envision a bronze statue of himself in a town square, perhaps in Havana, or Montgomery. He chose not to think of the pigeons roosting on his outstretched arms.

At a minimum, he estimated the initial formation of the new country would take only two Southern states and one Caribbean island. When other potential members of this fledgling republic saw what a success it was, they'd rush to join—provided their human lust for power was placated by giving the state officials high offices in the new administration. Younger, more diplomatic men in his castle were already working on this part of the plan. Two of them were even drafting a model constitution.

His hand reached automatically for one of the slim, rum-flavored cigars in his shirt pocket. The cigar was halfway to his lips before he was conscious of his action. He hesitated. He'd promised himself he wouldn't smoke until at least after the midday meal. It was his feeble effort to cut back. But the damage had been done by years of puffing, so what could it hurt to continue, unabated, now? He gripped the tobacco in his teeth and struck a wooden match on the porch railing to light up, blowing a satisfying cloud of aromatic smoke into the air. Personal weakness. Rationalization. But weren't all men and women weak in some way? Flawed human nature since Eden. It was the reason for all the conflict in the world. It was the reason he was doing his best to establish an independent political nation out of the ruins of the last war. Slavery was no longer an issue, yet he firmly believed economic forces without the help of enforced labor would allow his plan to succeed.

He took a satisfying puff on his cigar and reflected it was always best not to become too introspective—not to delve too deeply into human motives, the design of the universe, the unknown will of the Almighty. It was like wading into a lake: the water became murkier as it deepened until a man was in danger of drowning. Stick to what one could know, and what he did best.

A slight movement interrupted his reverie. His boots *thumped* down off the porch railing and he leaned forward, straining to see. He fumbled in his vest pocket for his spectacles. Through the smudged lenses, he focused on three horsemen emerging from the treeline. He rose from the rocker, flipped his half-smoked cigar away, and stepped down off the porch into the sunshine, vanity causing him to pocket the glasses.

When the riders came closer, a wave of relief swept over him as he recognized Nellie riding between two men. He knew the figure on the left in the straw hat and overalls. It was that eccentric hermit who lived a few miles away. The third rider, a big man, was a stranger to him.

He stood with quiet dignity while the riders reined up and dismounted. "Good to see you back safe and sound, Nellie," he said. "I was beginning to get concerned." He hesitated to embrace her in front of these men.

His granddaughter glanced quickly at her two companions, as if for assistance, then said: "Maybe you won't be so glad to see me when you hear what I have to say."

"Don't tell me that damned Canadian bank wouldn't let you have the money."

"No, sir. I would've telegraphed you had that been the case."

He studied her grim expression and felt a sinking sensation in his mid-section. Something had gone terribly wrong.

"We got robbed," she blurted out. "The two hundred and fifty thousand dollars is gone."

The shock he'd anticipated was only momentary, and his thoughts jumped immediately to the Claytons. "Come on up out of the sun," he said, turning his back so she couldn't read his face while he led the way up onto the shaded porch. He motioned them to the scattered chairs, then leaned his buttocks against the porch railing. "Perhaps this is something we should discuss in private," he said.

"They know all about it, Grandpa," Nellie said. "I think you know Uncle Billy," she went on quickly. "He moved into the old Hinton place over the ridge."

"Yes."

"And this is Kent Rasmussen, a former North-

West Mounted Policeman." She turned to Kent. "This is my grandfather, Silas Newburn."

The two men shook hands, Silas experiencing a slight uneasiness when he felt the strong grip and looked into the blue eyes. Some instinct told him this man was probably dangerous. But he said nothing as he leaned back against a porch post, arms folded, his emotions well in check now, awaiting Nellie's story.

"I hired Sergeant Rasmussen . . . Kent . . . to protect me and the money on my trip home," she began.

"Why?" He realized he sounded abrupt, like some angry schoolmaster.

"I'd spotted Johnny Clayton on the same train, going north, so I figured he was likely following me."

Silas waited in silence.

"Turned out, I was right. On the way back, he almost got away with the money in Chicago, but Kent was able to get it back and run him off. Wounded Johnny." She glanced up, fear showing in her eyes. She got up and paced nervously, wringing her hands, tears welling in her eyes.

Rasmussen cleared his throat. "Mister Newburn, what happened was this . . . I underestimated Johnny. . . ."

Silas held up a hand for silence. "Let her tell it." He wasn't going to make it easy.

She looked miserable, but seemed to gather herself, raised her head, and related the story of their loss, leaving out no detail.

Silas said nothing for at least a half minute after she'd finished, looking from one to the other.

"I got us a little turned around, and we wound up at Uncle Billy's place last night," she concluded. "He kindly let us stay the night, and then guided us over the ridge this morning."

Silas had a strong hunch that this Rasmussen fellow had somehow been involved in the loss. So far, there was not a shred of evidence for this belief. But he'd learned over many years to trust his instincts about people, especially when Yankees or outlanders were involved.

During this recitation, Uncle Billy had produced his briar from the pocket of his overalls, packed, and lighted it. In the silence that followed the story, he rose, and tapped the dottle out against a porch post. "Time for me to be gettin' home," he said. "I wish ya luck findin' your money. If I can be of help, you just send somebody to fetch me," he said, putting on his straw hat. He nodded a farewell, and stepped off the porch to mount his mule.

Silas watched him ride away, but his mind was elsewhere. What to do next? He turned back to Rasmussen who was still seated, hat on the floor next to his chair. "You say you talked to Johnny in the dining car the morning after you shot him?" he asked, trying to keep his tone neutral, not giving away his suspicions.

"That's right, sir."

"Tell me what you talked about."

He listened with his eyes, as well as his ears, to see if he could detect any hints from Rasmussen's manner that the man might be lying.

"Johnny gave no indication of what he was planning?" Silas asked. "I know Johnny Clayton pretty well. It's not like him to be bested like that, even shot, without being resentful."

"Actually, I thought I had him cowed," Rasmussen said. "I don't recall that he made any threats."

"Johnny's sneaky. He'll put his tail between his legs and let on he's whipped. Suckered you into thinking you'd seen the worst, or the last of him." He had trouble keeping the sneer out of his voice.

"I'm sorry, Mister Newburn. I wasn't on my toes. It's all my fault, and I'll be glad to do whatever I can to work with the sheriff to recover your money."

"Doubt anything can be done now. That cash has likely been split up among many of the Clayton clan already." He studied Rasmussen's face for any reaction, and detected no contrition. He was either very good at hiding his feelings, or he wasn't sorry at all. Rasmussen and Clayton could have easily plotted to rob his granddaughter.

"Why didn't you just get on the train and return home from Lebanon after the robbery?" Silas asked.

Rasmussen shrugged. "Felt it was my duty to at least see Nellie safely home."

And maybe meet up with Johnny Clayton for your share of the cash, Silas thought.

"Did you pay this man for his services?" Silas asked Nellie.

"I gave him five hundred dollars, which he offered to return. Promised him another five hundred when we got here safely with the money, to be paid out of the eight thousand dollars I was to receive," she replied.

But he saw a way to get a lot more than that without appearing to be a criminal, Silas thought.

Nellie looked to be on the verge of tears. "Is there anything I can do to make it up to you?"

"Not unless you have a quarter million dollars in your reticule."

Her lips compressed and she dropped her eyes under his gaze.

He looked back at Rasmussen. "You seem a bit young to have been in the war."

"I was only twelve when it ended."

At least you didn't fight for the Yankees, then, he thought.

"He's a Copperhead," Nellie said, her tone hopeful.

"A Southern sympathizer?" Silas was confused. This didn't fit with his early assessment of the man.

"At least his father was," she continued. "Show him your badge, Kent."

Rasmussen produced the altered copper penny.

"Haven't seen one of these in years," Silas said, examining the worn head of Liberty cut from a large cent. The others he recalled had varied in hand-made configurations. He turned it over and saw specks of solder where a pin had probably been attached.

"Are you a Copperhead?" he asked pointedly, handing back the badge.

"My father was. There's no such thing any more. This is just a keepsake."

"I suppose that's right," Silas said softly, realizing that this big, strapping man, approaching middle age, had been only a child during the terrible war that still seemed so real, that had done so much to shape his own life. With a pang of regret, he sensed how he must appear to these young people—a relic of time gone by, a living spokesman for history that was no longer relevant. This thought generated frustration and anger, making him even more determined to accomplish his goals—and quickly.

"Nellie, show your friend to one of the spare rooms upstairs."

"Yes, Grandpa," she said, sounding relieved at the change of subject.

"You'll accept our hospitality by dining with us

this evening and staying the night before you start back," he said to Rasmussen.

"You don't want me to stay and help you recover your money?" Rasmussen asked, rising from his chair.

"That's a family matter and we'll deal with it ourselves," Silas said.

"Grandpa, after we rest up, I'd like to take him into Springfield and show him around town," she said.

"Suit yourself. But stay clear of the Claytons. I don't want any trouble until I decide what to do about this." He hesitated. "Before you go anywhere, I want to have a private talk with you . . . out by the barn."

"Yes, sir."

He retrieved his hat from the hall tree inside the door. It was time to call an emergency meeting of his castle.

In years gone by, when there'd been a few slaves about the place, his wife would have had the house staff busy gathering selected summer vegetables from the garden and laying out the china and silver for a dinner guest, while she decided what meat to prepare for supper. Silas would have called for the stable boy to saddle his horse and bring him around to the front porch. But now there was no wife, no slaves—not even a garden. He hardly gave those vanished times a thought as he strode to the barn.

Nellie was already there, looking apprehensive.

Standing in the shade, he questioned her thoroughly about the trip. He probed into minute details of how she'd met Rasmussen, what he'd said, how he'd acted, how long he'd been out of her sight on the train, whether or not he'd gotten off, however briefly, at any stop along the way. By the time he finished his examination, he was more convinced than ever that this blond stranger was involved in robbing his granddaughter. He bluntly told her of his strong suspicions, and turned a deaf ear to her protests as he went into the barn and saddled his tall, sleek bay. He'd ride to town and notify as many of the dozen knights of his castle as he could locate on short notice.

Swinging into the saddle with accustomed ease, he turned his horse toward Springfield. The tension in his stomach was similar to the feeling he used to have just before a horse race. He sensed, for better or worse, tonight's meeting would go far in deciding the eventual fate of the Newburn and Clayton families.

Chapter Eight

A three-quarter moon was peeking through the leaves of the trees when Silas Newburn dismounted, loosened the saddle girth, and looped the reins around the hitching rail. Nearby crickets ceased their monotonous *chirping* when he *jangled* his key ring and fumbled in the dark to unlock the door of the stone meeting hall of his castle. Since he held the office of Grand Knight, he always made it a point to arrive early and set up things for the others.

Just inside, he struck a match to a coal-oil lantern fashioned from a human skull and held it aloft to light his way from the anteroom into the larger inner chamber. Here, he replaced the eerie light of the death's head lantern by touching a long, lighted taper to the overhead chandelier.

The room was stuffy, so he opened the back door to admit some of the humid night air. Thirty years earlier, to ensure secrecy, the building had been constructed with no windows.

Silas carried the skull lantern back into the anteroom where a row of hooks held the hoods and gowns of the knights. He donned his crimson robe, trimmed at the sleeves and neck in gold, then slipped the pointed hood over his head and adjusted the eyeholes. Leaving the death's head lantern burning for the others, he returned to the inner chamber and lit ten thick candles that stood in flat brass holders, one in front of each chair along the table. Beside each candle was a wooden-handled snuffer, the business end of which was crafted into the figure of a snake, nose to tail, forming a small golden circle, symbol of their order.

Everything was in place and he pulled out his Elgin. He had a few minutes yet, so he stepped out the back door for a cigar. In times past, an armed guard with a dog patrolled the ground around the castle during convocations to prevent raucous disruption or outright attack from the younger members of the Clayton clan. But now, no one seemed to care that a dwindling group of middle-aged men still met in what was no more than a lodge hall. No longer were the Knights of the Golden Circle a force with power stronger and more sinister than even the law itself. During the years since the war, many of the knights had ceased to attend the convocations, many had died, or moved west, and younger men were more difficult to recruit. In an effort to keep the organization relevant, Silas and a few of his long-deceased contemporaries had streamlined the ritual. No longer was the oath of allegiance chanted in unison. They now used their secret handshake merely as a sign of recognition away from the castle when strangers were around. They still wore the hooded robes at meetings to show they were knights—one, unconquerable, and forever defiant. The ceremonial garb provided a sense of solemn dignity and the hoods also gave them a sense, however tenuous, of anonymity.

His hood draped over one arm, he puffed his

cigar and stared up through the leafy branches at the silvery moon, savoring the moment without thinking ahead to what he had to say at the meeting. The right words would come when he needed them; they always did.

When he'd stopped at the sawmill to tell his oldest son Martin about the meeting, Martin had mentioned seeing Johnny Clayton in town. This hadn't surprised Silas, since he knew Johnny would have to strut and preen after so big a heist. But Martin's next remark had startled Silas and confirmed his earlier suspicions. "Dad, Johnny had a bunch of his armed friends with him, like they were looking for trouble. And I saw him talking to a stranger . . . a big blond man."

"Was Nellie there?" Silas had asked, holding his breath as he waited for the answer.

"No."

Silas had paused, looking down at his son who was wiping away the sawdust sticking to his sweaty forearms.

"Good," he finally had said, turning his bay to ride off. "See you tonight."

Now his reverie was interrupted by the *thudding* of horsemen approaching the front of the building. He ground out the butt of his cigar under his boot heel, slid the hood over his head, and reentered the building, closing the back door behind him.

The last of the hooded figures entered the inner chamber and seated themselves at the long table. A *scuffing* of boots and chairs was the only sound. No one spoke. From a slightly raised dais, Silas Newburn sat facing them in his large wooden chair carved with a knight's head. He knew each man as well as if he could see his face—the stooped form of

Horace Bigelow; Thomson's barrel shape that pushed against the loose robe; Hutter, whose ceremonial garb had not been washed in months; the confident swing of his own son Martin; the broad-shouldered form of his oldest son, Tad; Connolly's blue eyes that shone in the candlelight through the vision holes cut in the hood. The others were all known to him, as he was to them.

A half minute of silence passed before he spoke. "Fellow knights, I wish first to apologize for pressing you to vote Nellie Newburn our courier. You've probably heard that on her way home from Canada, she was set upon and robbed by Johnny Clayton. I take full responsibility for the loss of that quarter million dollars."

The hoods prevented his assessing their reaction. He stood up and let the loose sleeves fall at his sides. "I called you here tonight so we can decide what to do about this outrage." He spoke slowly, somberly, forming his thoughts as he went. "As you know, a state of animosity, if not of war, has existed between the Newburn and Clayton families since I was very young. There is no need to rake up all those past injuries . . . you are well aware of them. As I see it, this act of armed aggression against my granddaughter and the stealing of a vast amount of money belonging to our Order . . . money that was to be used in the furtherance of our goals of a new country . . . is properly punishable by death. Only a violent reaction to such atrocities can impress the Claytons with the gravity of their crime, and put the fear of God and the knights into them."

He paused to allow his words to sink in. The hooded figures at the table might have been ten graven images—not a sound, not a movement.

"I have good reason to believe this act was carried out successfully only with the help of another man, a stranger among us. My granddaughter unwisely employed him as a guard to accompany her home. He is a big-boned, blond man, more than six feet tall, who goes by the name of Kent Rasmussen."

Silas paused again, feeling the perspiration beginning to trickle down his face under the stifling hood. He opened and closed his hands, palms moist.

"For the good of our Order and its ultimate aims, we must recover our money before it's dispersed. By striking hard and fast, we can stun this clan into submission, and threaten them with annihilation if they do not give up the stolen fortune. I believe we must start with the leaders. If the head of the snake is severed, it cannot live. Johnny Clayton and Kent Rasmussen contain the fangs of this two-headed serpent. They must die!" He stopped, his declaration ringing in the following silence. This time he waited a full minute before he spoke again. "What say you?"

This time the hooded men turned, one to another, but still no one spoke aloud. They seemed to be communicating with eyes alone, or some body language since two or three gravely nodded.

Silas gave them time to consider. Then: "We will vote. There are ten of you. As usual, a majority of seven is required for a decision. If you vote to allow these men to live, you will signify by allowing your candle to remain lighted. If, on the other hand, you vote for their execution, you will snuff your candle with the golden circle in front of you." He looked up and down the table. "Does anyone wish to say anything before we vote?"

Silence.

"Proceed to cast your vote."

Almost as one, the circular golden snakes were raised and all ten candles were extinguished. Thin, twisting wisps of white smoke curled upward into the light of the overhead chandelier.

"Fellow knights, you have spoken. So be it."

Kent Rasmussen pushed back from the dining room table in the Newburn house. "That was delicious!" He sighed. "Among your other talents, you can cook."

Nellie smiled. "It's about the only thing I do well. Since Grandma died and I came back here to live, after Johnny and I split, I took over the household duties." She shrugged. "Somebody had to. Grandpa could get along without me, but he won't hire anyone to cook or clean. And when he's here alone, he doesn't eat right, like a lot of old people."

"Where is he tonight?"

"At one of those meetings of the knights, or the Sons of Liberty, or whatever they're calling themselves these days," she said, carrying two bowls into the adjacent kitchen.

Rasmussen was uneasy around Silas and felt relieved the old man was absent so he could spend this last evening with Nellie before he headed home. He got up to help her clear the table and put away the leftover food. "That pumpkin pie with thick cream was the perfect ending to a perfect meal."

She gave him a curious look. "That wasn't pumpkin. This is the wrong time of year for pumpkins. That was sweet potato pie."

"I've heard of that. In fact, I once saw some Confederate paper money with a picture of some general eating sweet potato pie. Sounded really strange to me at the time and I wondered what it tasted like."

She opened the stove and thrust in several pieces of kindling and set a kettle of water to heat for washing dishes.

He'd noticed that she busied herself with cooking and serving, commenting on the food, the heat, pouring him more coffee—anything, it seemed, to keep the conversation light. Yet, he sensed her depression beneath the gaiety.

The dishes stacked and the water heating, they lounged in the living room. A coal-oil lamp glowed on a marble-top table by the front window. June bugs *buzzed* against the screen door.

She seemed preoccupied as she sat on the horsehair sofa, legs drawn up under her. Rasmussen slouched in an upholstered chair, legs sprawled out comfortably.

"I hate to see you leave," she finally said, breaking a long silence.

"Your grandpa made it pretty clear he doesn't want me around."

Another silence as she stared at her hands in her lap.

"What do you think will happen?" she asked, not looking up.

"I wish I knew. You know your family and the people here."

"Doubt the money will ever be found. But Grandpa and my uncles and the rest of that bunch who call themselves the Knights of the Golden Circle will try to kill Johnny. And that will set off this war between our families again."

"Again? Has it ever stopped?"

"Not really." Her lips compressed. "But it'll get worse now. I'm almost sorry I got you into this. Now I've come to depend on you, to value your company. And you'll be leaving tomorrow."

"We could keep in touch." Even as he said it, he realized it would be nearly impossible. He began to regret leaving as well. Nellie was a beautiful, intelligent woman who'd crossed his path even before he was off active duty. He'd invested time and effort in her welfare—and failed miserably. Human curiosity made him want to stay and help if he could, and at least see the outcome of all this. The outline of a plan began to form. "I'll return our horses to the Lebanon livery," he said. "Then I'll catch the train back to Springfield and get a hotel room."

She seemed to brighten a little, then her face fell again. "I'd love to know you were close by, but Grandpa would surely find out."

"That visit to your Sheriff Bixby was a waste of time today," he said, changing the subject.

"I knew it would be. But we had to report the robbery."

"He had an easy excuse for doing nothing. Said if a robbery like that had actually taken place, it was in Laclede County, and he had no jurisdiction outside of Greene County. Maybe we should report it to the sheriff in Lebanon," he added.

"If you're going back that way to return the rented horses, you can do it," she said without enthusiasm. "I'm sure it will be only a formality. From what I've heard, that sheriff is as useless as Bixby."

"One thing I didn't tell you," he began, wondering if he should even mention it now. "After we visited the sheriff's office and you stopped at the market to buy meat for supper, I went down the street for a beer."

She nodded.

"Ran into Johnny Clayton and a few of his cronies in the saloon."

"What?" She went suddenly pale.

"They were having a helluva time. Loud and laughing. But it got quiet when I walked in. They were sitting at tables and I just stood at the bar and kept my hands in plain sight 'cause they were all well armed. It was about then I decided I wasn't thirsty, after all, and left. They followed me outside and cut off my retreat. 'It'd be a waste of time going to the sheriff,' Johnny told me.

" 'Already found that out,' I said.

" 'If you got good sense, you'll clear out of Missouri.' He pushed up close to me. With that hand still bandaged, I knew he couldn't go for his gun. But he had at least six friends who looked like they were hoping I would go for mine."

"Lord! Of all the gall!" she said. "And right there in public, too. But that's Johnny for you. I wouldn't have expected anything else. If anybody saw you talking, and word gets back to Grandpa . . . which it will . . . he'll be more convinced than ever that you and Johnny were in on this robbery together." She bit her lip.

"Your grandpa thinks I was in on the robbery?" He was stunned.

"Yes. He got me aside and questioned me about you and all the details of our trip. He's got it in his head that you and Johnny were in cahoots."

"Damn! No wonder Silas seemed so cool to me. It wasn't just because I was a stranger."

She nodded. "Y'know, Johnny was right . . . it's better you go, and not look back. Get away and go home, and forget you ever heard of me or my kin."

"Forget I ever met you? Not likely." He said it with more feeling than he intended. She looked up and smiled, a tear glistening on her cheek and her face glowing in the soft light of the low-burning lamp.

In that moment, he resolved to find a way to become her unseen guardian angel.

Approaching hoof beats sounded through the open doorway.

"Grandpa's back. I recognize that bay's gait."

Rasmussen got up. "Then I'll say good night and go to my room." Hearing the horse go behind the house to the stable, he came and gave her a hug. She clung to him for several seconds.

"The water's hot. I better get to those dishes, then fix Grandpa's supper. I'll see you at breakfast." She turned toward the kitchen.

Rasmussen climbed the darkened stairway to his second-floor guest room. No need to antagonize the old man with any unnecessary contact. Tomorrow he'd be out of here. Maybe some plan would occur to him after a good night's sleep.

Rasmussen slept soundly without dreaming. When he opened his eyes, he was lying on his back, head turned toward the open window beside his bed. The fresh scent of early dawn in the outdoors greeted him. He fumbled for the watch in his vest pocket that hung on the bed post. 5:06a.m. An early start was in order, before Nellie got up. He hated tearful good byes. Stretching mightily, he swung his legs over the side of the bed.

Five minutes later, he was descending the creaking

stairs, saddlebags slung over one shoulder, Merwin-
Hulbert strapped to his waist. He would have welcomed a cup of coffee, but that could wait. Time to
slip away quietly.

As he opened the door and stepped onto the front
porch, he was startled to see Nellie, fully dressed,
sitting in one of the rockers.

"I was hoping to slide out without waking you,"
he said.

"Thought you might."

"Where's your grandpa Silas?"

"Up and gone an hour ago."

"These Newburns are an early rising bunch."

"He had something on his mind," she remarked,
glancing at him in the gray light. "He was in a rush.
Slugged down a glass of water, grabbed a cold bis-
cuit, and took off."

"There's enough light for me to find my way back
over that short cut Uncle Billy showed us," he said.
"I can't go wrong . . . over the ridge and hold a
steady northeast heading by the sun. I'll eventually
bisect the main Springfield road, and then just turn
right toward Lebanon."

"You got it. That'll save you riding out of your
way through Springfield." She got up and came to
his side. "I've got the coffee boiling."

"In a few minutes. Come. While I saddle up, we
can talk."

Forty minutes later, as the sun was slanting
obliquely across the open meadow in front of the big
house, Rasmussen turned in his saddle and waved to
the woman on the porch. Then he faced forward,
gripped the long tether of the trailing horse, and followed the rutted road into the dimness of the thick
woods. He sighed. It would be a long, lonely ride to

Lebanon, but he had no intention of continuing on north to Minnesota—at least not until he'd seen this business through. He hadn't quite been able get a handle on his feelings for Nellie Newburn. In a way, he felt protective of her as a younger sister. Yet, in another—yes, in another, she was a desirable, experienced woman who'd seen the rougher side of life, but hadn't lost her wit or the softer side of her nature. And damned fine-looking, into the bargain, he thought with a smile.

Three hours later he'd managed to urge his mount, slipping and sliding, up and over the steep wooded ridge. He reined up just on the downhill side and dismounted. Time to let his mount blow, and maybe switch to the spare horse. He was sweating in the humid heat of mid-morning, the sun bearing down on him in the small clearing. He scuffed through the leaf mold, and reached down to loosen the saddle girth.

The *boom* of a big-caliber rifle blasted the stillness and something slammed into the left side of his back. He spun and fell sideways, striking his head. An explosion of bright lights in his vision. Then, blackness.

Chapter Nine

When Rasmussen opened his eyes, he had no idea how long he'd been out—thirty seconds? Thirty minutes? Unconsciousness had briefly spared him from the nauseating pain in his head and left shoulder blade that now swept over him in waves. He lay on his back where he'd fallen, filtering the sun's rays through the screen of his eyelashes, breathing slowly, willing away the pain. If he moved, it would be worse. What'd happened? Had he been clubbed? Shot? Fragments began tumbling into place. Had he imagined the *boom* of a rifle simultaneous with the blow? He recalled being conscious as he pitched forward. Must've struck his head against the tree beside him. In addition to the ache in his head, his ear and cheek burned as if he'd scraped them against rough bark.

Had he been dealing with fractious mules and gotten careless, he could've been kicked this hard, but that wasn't the case with these docile horses that were ripping up mouthfuls of grass nearby. This had been a deliberate human attack from ambush. Whoever had done this might still be watching to make sure he was dead. So he didn't move, preferring to gather his wits and strength. An instant before the shot came, he'd bent forward, reaching for the cinch. That slight movement had evidently thrown off the shooter's aim by a few inches, or the bullet would have caught him squarely in the back and likely been fatal. As it was, by looking down, he could see no blood on the front of his shirt. But there was a burning sensation in his back near the shoulder. He could feel wetness soaking his shirt, and sensed flies *buzzing* near his head and settling on fresh blood by his collar. He knew he must staunch the flow, but delayed sitting up to assess his condition. One more shot from a watching gunman could finish him. His left forearm pressed against a lump at his waist, so he knew his loaded revolver still rested in its cross-draw position. If anyone came close, he might have a fighting chance.

His head and shoulder settled into a dull ache as he concentrated on listening to the peaceful *chirping* of the birds in the trees. He began to itch from the grass and perspiration, and finally decided he had to take a chance on sitting up. He rolled over and pushed himself up with his good arm, pausing to allow a wave of nausea to pass. Then he crawled to the base of the tree and sat with his right side resting against the trunk, out of direct sunlight. Sweat ran down his sides under his arms and also tickled his face.

Suddenly he heard hoofs *clomping* through dead leaves and undergrowth. He drew his Merwin-Hulbert with his right hand and scanned the thickening green of the deep woods for any sign of a rider. The sounds ceased for a moment. Then the *squeak* of saddle leather told him someone was dismounting. Slow, cautious footsteps of a man *crunched* dry leaves. He couldn't twist far enough to his left to see who was coming. He leaned back in the shelter of the trunk and held his gun.

"By God!" a voice rasped.

Rasmussen swung up his revolver.

"Don't shoot! It's me . . . Uncle Billy!"

The old man stepped into full view, sweeping the clearing with a cocked Remington. Then he hunkered by Rasmussen. "Heard a shot. You see who it was?" he husked, just above a whisper.

"No. Son-of-a-bitch ambushed me." Just the effort of talking made him giddy. He hoped he hadn't lost too much blood.

"Probably skedaddled," the old man said, "thinking you're a goner." He eased Rasmussen forward, then took a knife and slit the bloody shirt across the top of the shoulder. He glanced at the wound, pursing his lips. "Can you move your arm a-tall?"

"Barely."

Uncle Billy gently probed the surrounding tissue. "Hmmm . . . the slug plowed a groove along your back from the bottom of the shoulder blade all the way to the top. Appears to have missed the bone."

In a mist of pain, Rasmussen felt relief, realizing the bullet had not lodged inside, or hit anything vital.

"Got a knot on your noggin, too, but that ain't gonna kill ya. You ain't seein' double, are ya? No? Good. Scuffed your face when you fell." He rocked back on his haunches and appeared to consider the situation. "Lemme find some moss to pack that long gash and stop the bleeding."

No sooner said than done. In a few minutes the old man had a double handful of cool moss pressed against the furrow, bound in place with Rasmussen's one spare shirt from his saddlebags.

"Reckon you can make it to my cabin? It's about a half mile."

Rasmussen nodded. "You're pretty damn' strong for an old coot," he gritted between clenched teeth as Uncle Billy half carried, half dragged him to his horse and boosted him into the saddle. Everything swam before Rasmussen's eyes with unnatural brightness as if he were about to pass out again. He leaned forward, gripping the saddle horn.

"Hold tight . . . or I can tie you on," Uncle Billy said.

"I'll make it." He would never let on he was about to faint.

The next ten minutes were an agony of pain and sickness as the old man rode his mule, leading Rasmussen's mount and the spare horse down through the timber, finally reining up at the shack. He nearly fell off his horse.

Uncle Billy helped him inside and onto the only bed. Then the old man left briefly to put up the stock in the stable with feed and water.

From blood loss and profuse sweating, Rasmussen was suffering an acute thirst. Uncle Billy came back and gave him water, then stripped off the bloody shirt and tossed it into a bucket. He removed the moss, cleaned the wounds with carbolic, and bound the shoulder firmly with clean white dish towels from the clothesline.

"Feeling some better?" he asked, washing his hands at the sink.

"Yeah."

"Leastwise you got a little more color to your face. Hard to tell, though, with whey-faced folks like you Scandinavians." He grinned.

Rasmussen was too weak for a sharp comeback.

"Best you rest a bit. Then we'll talk," Uncle Billy said, then turned to his cupboard and got down three small bottles, and proceeded to mix some concoction in a tin cup. "Here, drink this. It'll dull the pain and help you sleep."

Rasmussen accepted and drank it down in three gulps. Whatever it was had a smooth, mellow taste and contained a measure of alcohol. For some reason, he trusted the old man. It wasn't as if he had a lot of choice, although he could have refused the concoction. But he doubted if the old man would have brought him to his cabin if he intended to poison him. Rasmussen had felt the hot-sick sting of bullets twice before during his years in the Mounted Police. By those standards, he judged this wound to be relatively minor. He'd be weak from shock and loss of blood but, barring infection, should pull through. Nevertheless, he hated to be laid up here for days. He assumed the would-be assassin knew these hills and woods. If the man were serious about finishing the job, this shack would likely be one of the first places he'd look. He couldn't allow this recluse to put himself in danger. The old man had probably saved his life, but Rasmussen couldn't stay. He determined to rest until dark, then take a horse and make camp somewhere in the woods without a fire.

His eyelids were growing heavy. A great weariness overcame all his limbs. He lay his head back on the stacked pillows. He'd rest a little, then be up and away.

When he awoke, it was dark, and Uncle Billy was dozing in a rocking chair near his bed. The only light in the shack was a coal-oil lamp burning, low, on the table in the other room, but visible from where he lay. His mouth was dry and he felt feverish. "Water," he managed to croak.

The old man was a light sleeper and immediately

moved, cat-like, into the other room, and came back with a crock pitcher of water and a tin cup. As Rasmussen gulped down cup after cup of the cool water, he knew he wasn't going anywhere for a while. His earlier plan for a quick getaway would have to be put aside. For better or worse, he was in the hermit's care and protection until he could get back on his feet.

Distorted, feverish nightmares followed. He lost all track of time. During brief intervals of wakefulness, he was conscious of the presence of Uncle Billy, sometimes lifting his head and spooning broth into his mouth, or laying soothing wet cloths on his burning forehead. He had such fearful dreams that he struggled to stay awake, but couldn't. Throbbing pain in his back brought him to consciousness to discover the old man swabbing the wound with some burning liquid and changing the dressing.

There followed what seemed a long blank time when he knew nothing. On opening his eyes, he knew immediately his fever had broken in profuse sweating. The old man wiped him off with a damp sponge and gave him a drink. Then Rasmussen drifted into a peaceful, restful sleep.

He came to. Daylight again. He felt much better, though weak and hungry.

Uncle Billy came into the room, carrying a calabash of water.

"Feeling better?"

"Yeah. How long have I been out?"

"Two days and two nights. Thought I was going to lose you there for a bit."

"My shoulder even feels like it's on the mend." He flexed his arm gingerly.

"It'll be stiff for a week or two. Maybe longer."

Rasmussen regarded the hermit with new respect. "What do I say to a man who just saved my life? You must have some medical training."

"No. Just some experience with bullet wounds. I did what I could to help Nature along. You apparently have a strong, healthy constitution."

"Next question is, how much longer?"

"I'll help you get on your feet right now. You'll be weak as a newborn kitten, but it's best you get moving, get all your parts working again. I'd guess you'll be here at least another day or two, though."

"Let's get at it, then."

The rest of that day, Rasmussen spent walking slowly, and resting, eating, and drinking small amounts. By evening, he was as exhausted as if he'd been doing farm labor for a week. The sun was hardly down before he was in bed, asleep.

He awoke the next morning, seventy-two hours after his wounding, feeling rested and refreshed. He could use his arm a little, and the furrow in his back had scabbed over and was healing nicely. After dressing, he sat down at the breakfast table with his host and benefactor. His appetite had returned with a vengeance. From the slack in his belt, he judged he'd lost at least ten pounds.

The two men hardly spoke as they stoked up on fried sowbelly, hominy, chunks of bread torn from the loaf, all washed down with strong coffee sweetened with molasses.

"I finally feel human again, thanks to you." Rasmussen sighed and pushed back from the table. He wondered if this was the time to broach his most pressing concern. "Has anyone been here since you brought me in?" he asked.

"Had one visitor, but I deflected him."

"Who was it?" He felt the hair prickle on the back of his neck.

"Blake Rogers."

"Name means nothing to me."

"First cousin to Johnny Clayton," Uncle Billy explained. "Big man. Might near as big as you. About forty. Ugly cuss. Nose busted a few times. One of the meanest of the lot."

"What'd he want? Me?"

Uncle Billy nodded. "He come on foot, carrying a big bore rifle. Figured he was looking for what was left of you. You was sound asleep and I slid you off and under the bed. Went out to meet him with my scatter-gun, like I do everybody who comes around. Played dumb. And I diverted him away from the stable."

"You think he's the one who shot me?"

"No doubt about it. Probably on orders."

"Why? I'm not part of this damned feud."

"You were Nellie's guard. That makes you one of the Newburns."

Rasmussen took a deep breath. "I had thought about staying. Felt bad for losing that money. You reckon Johnny Clayton thought I was a threat and tried to have me eliminated? Or was he just out for revenge because I shot him in the hand?"

"I don't have the answers to those questions," the old man said, getting up to refill both their coffee cups.

"That description of Blake Rogers sounds a lot like one of the men who robbed us at Lebanon."

"I asked him what he was after. Said he was out hunting, winged a deer and was trailing it by the blood. Likely a lie. Most folks hereabouts hunt deer in the fall. But I didn't say nothing. Just told him I hadn't seen no deer. Just stood there while he shuffled around, tryin' to think of some excuse to get into my place. Wanted a drink of water, and I pointed out the spring on the hill. He had a slug o' water, then took off down yonder toward the road. He never come back this way, and that was two day ago."

"You haven't had much sleep while I've been in your bed," Rasmussen observed.

"A solid nine or ten hours tonight will set me right."

"Then I'll clear outta here and make sure you don't have to protect me from discovery."

The old man looked at him steadily for a moment without speaking. Then he said: "You were gonna throw in with the Newburns?"

"From what Nellie said, I'm considered the enemy by her grandpa Silas as well, so I'm anathema to both sides." He took a deep breath. "After I return these horses to the Lebanon livery, I might slip back here and see if I can convince Nellie to leave. And, while I'm here, I might try sticking a burr under the Claytons' saddles, too."

Uncle Billy continued to stare at him, a thoughtful frown on his face. Finally he got up and paced around the small room. "Believe this thing between the Newburns and Claytons is coming to a head."

"Wouldn't doubt it, after that robbery."

"Even before that, the pot was starting to boil." He paused. "You were a sergeant in the Canadian Mounted Police."

"That's right."

"Why'd you leave it?"

"Got tired. Wanted to try something else."

"Would you consider puttin' your lawman's skills back to work?"

Rasmussen glanced up sharply. "What?"

"You strike me as trustworthy. May I tell you something in strict confidence?"

"Of course."

"I'm not Uncle Billy, the half-cracked hermit and treasure hunter, folks around here believe I am. My real name is Alex Thorne, retired Secret Service agent."

Rasmussen felt his eyes widen. Was this man completely delusional? Maybe the result of too much whiskey and solitude?

"I can see you don't believe me. I understand that." With a stove lid handle he pried up a foot-long section of floorboard near the table. Reaching through the opening, he withdrew a small tin box and opened it. "My identification papers and badge," he said, handing the box to Rasmussen. "You'll also find an official letter from the Secretary of the Treasury calling me back from retirement for a special assignment. That assignment is to infiltrate these former Rebel diehards and locate the vast treasure they supposedly have hidden. We've had reports the Knights of the Golden Circle plan to create another civil disturbance, and use this treasure to again split the United States."

As Uncle Billy spoke, he seemed to lose his backwoods dialect.

Rasmussen scanned the official-looking documents and the badge. "How do I know you didn't steal this stuff to assume someone else's identity?"

"Good question. There's a photograph of me taken less than two years ago."

Rasmussen found the picture attached to an identification card. He studied the image—an unmistakable likeness. He looked up.

"I'm a little grayer now, and I grew this beard when I came to the Ozarks," Thorne said. "Figured by playing the part of a harmless old coot, nobody would give me a second look."

"Why're you telling me this?"

"If you were going to put your hand into this feud anyway, I thought you might want to work with me, instead."

"You're trying to keep the old man, Silas Newburn, and his knights from getting that cold cache and using it to form a new political entity, taking part of the old South with him?"

"Exactly."

"As I understand the situation, the Clayton family wants all that stash to split among their relatives. So you're actually working on the side of the Claytons, figuring if they get the money, no harm will be done?"

"No. I'm not working for either side. Much of that money was stolen Union payrolls, or cash from bank robberies or train hold-ups by various outlaw gangs since the war. The United States government will confiscate it. What can be identified will be returned . . . what can't will go into the general treasury as belated spoils of war."

Rasmussen was silent, trying to absorb this flood of new information.

"Because of the bitterness remaining from Reconstruction, and the bitterness of this family feud, hatreds are going to flare into killings. This is not just a treasure hunt. This is deadly serious business . . . as you found out the other day."

"I don't want anything to happen to Nellie."

"I don't, either. I suspected you were sweet on her."

"She told me she was disgusted with this whole business and wants nothing to do with it. But, by accident of birth, she is part of it. Tried to convince her to leave here and start another life, but she said she couldn't bring herself to run away."

"Sometimes our loyalties can be the death of us."

Rasmussen pondered the wisdom of this statement. This Uncle Billy, who'd just transmogrified into secret agent, Alex Thorne, had saved his life. He owed the man everything; he couldn't just walk away.

"I'll work with you." He held out his hand. "Tell me the plan." Committing himself, he felt the stab of danger in his gut. Loyalty to this mission might, indeed, be the death of them.

Chapter Ten

Nellie Newburn was sitting in a front porch rocker, writing an entry in her journal when she heard the shot. She looked up from the open volume in her lap. A large bore rifle, she guessed, probably two miles distant. Accustomed from childhood to hearing the discharge of hunters' guns echoing through these hills, she could identify most weapons by sound alone. Maybe someone shooting a varmint, she thought. But nobody she knew would be hunting rabbit or squirrel or deer this time of year unless they were really hungry.

She took up her pen and journal, but then paused, curiosity tugging at the back of her mind. That wasn't the pop of a .22, or even the sharp crack of a .30-30—more of a heavy, loud boom, like a .45- or .50-caliber. Because of the history of violence between the families, she was always apprehensive when she heard shots. This was only one shot, so it wasn't someone taking target practice. It'd come from the northeast where the long ridge lifted a barrier between their land and Uncle Billy's cabin beyond. As far as she knew, the old hermit didn't own a rifle. She'd noticed only a shotgun and the old percussion Remington. She laid the book down again. The only person in these parts who favored a big rifle like that was Blake Rogers, known to the Newburns as Black Rogers. His pride and joy was an 1886 model Winchester .45, good for nothing but hunting large animals—or men. If that was Rogers, he could be shooting at anything just for the pleasure of it. He was as mean as he was crazy. Wild boar roamed these hills, so maybe he was taking on quarry that was nearer his own size for a change. He raised a few cattle and hogs, so didn't need to hunt his meat.

She put the gunshot out of her thoughts and concentrated on her journal. She'd carried it on her trip, but made only intermittent entries. The velvet-covered volume was like an intimate companion to whom she could address her innermost thoughts and feelings without fear of being misunderstood or chastised for what she said. She needed a confidant. Kent Rasmussen had come close to filling that rôle, but now he was gone, and she was disconsolate. Intuition told her that he was in no way involved with her estranged husband in plotting the robbery. She couldn't imagine why her grandfather was so persistent in accusing him of complicity. She'd never known Grandpa Silas to be afraid of anything, but perhaps it was easier for him to blame an outsider than to take on Johnny, who had the backing of the whole Clayton clan. There had to come a time when a man quit fighting and succumbed to the tranquility of old age. She fervently wished that time were now.

She dipped her pen in the tiny ink bottle on the floor beside the chair and continued writing. Ten minutes later she closed the book, stoppered the bottle, and went inside. Time to prepare lunch, in case Grandpa came home. She didn't know where he'd gone—possibly to play cards with his cronies in their favorite saloon in town. But he'd acted differently since she'd arrived home with the bad news. He'd been like a man on a mission, coming and going at odd hours, acting very distracted, ignoring her presence, except for his initial questioning about her trip and Kent Rasmussen. He probably had no time for cards now. Whatever was afoot, she'd hear about it soon enough.

Pausing in the kitchen, she wondered what to fix for lunch. Maybe a pot of potato soup with crumbled bacon in it. That would keep if he didn't come home soon.

As it turned out, Grandpa Silas didn't come home for lunch, or supper, either. He'd still not arrived when she took the lamp and climbed the stairs to her room at eleven that night. She'd long ago ceased to worry about his comings and goings. There was no point in being concerned for his safety. He'd led a rough life and survived to age seventy-eight without her help.

Nellie didn't fall asleep right away, and was just drifting off, sometime later, when she heard the downstairs door open and close, then muffled voices. Rousing to full wakefulness, she slid out of bed, reached for her dressing gown on the chair, and padded softly to the bedroom door.

She recognized her grandfather's voice, then another man's, pitched somewhat lower. They were obviously trying to be quiet. After a couple of muffled exchanges, she picked out the voice of her Uncle Thaddeus—Tad—Silas's middle son. Her curiosity satisfied, she started to return to bed.

A match flared, briefly dispersing the dense darkness of the foyer as Silas lit a cigar. Then blackness closed in again, and Silas said: "Make sure you do it as quietly as you can. I don't want word of this leaking out until we leave."

In spite of her habitual aversion to eavesdropping, she caught herself pausing to listen. She didn't catch Uncle Tad's response.

"No . . . no nitro," Silas countered. "Too risky to transport. Bring one case of dynamite and blasting caps. That should do the job."

"That's bound to arouse suspicion," Tad said.

"Just buy a little here and there around town. Ride over to the hardware in Lebanon if you have to. Anybody should ask, we're blowing stumps out here on my place."

Tad must have turned away, so she didn't catch his reply.

"Five picked men . . . ," Silas was saying ". . . by train through. . . ."

She strained to hear, creeping outside her doorway and crouching behind the balustrade. They were going somewhere by train, carrying explosives. She missed the next exchange as the two men moved back under the overhang. Her stomach tensed and she hardly dared breathe. Not only would she be embarrassed to be caught eavesdropping, but no telling what her grandfather might do to her. She was in enough trouble already.

The hall clock began to chime, then struck one. She couldn't hear more without exposing her presence. She caught the familiar scent of fresh cigar smoke drifting up the stairway. It was not unpleasant. Only when the stogies grew rank did she object to their strong odor.

The two men moved toward the front door. She couldn't hear their words, but the timbre of their voices indicated Tad was leaving. She soundlessly scuttled back to her bedroom door and halted, the polished wood floor cool under her bare feet.

The front door opened. Then: "At least we're rid of that Yankee who helped Johnny Clayton relieve Nellie of our cash," Silas said.

"Yeah. I heard he left."

Silas chuckled. "Better than that. I got word from old man Clayton himself that one of theirs put away that blond bastard for good."

Nellie nearly cried out. She caught her breath and clutched the door frame.

"Why?" Tad asked.

"That Rasmussen must've had a falling out with Johnny," Silas said. "No honor among thieves, I reckon. Besides, he could've brought back a federal marshal . . . stirred up a real stink here."

"He's one less the Claytons will have to split that quarter million with," Tad said.

"They had no idea they were doing our job for us," Silas said. Then the sound of the screen door being pushed open, and the two men moved out onto the porch.

Nellie crept to the railing again.

"We'll make a run around the Claytons," she could hear her grandfather saying. "While they're distracted splitting up the stolen cash and preparing to fight us, we take our best men and go for the big cache. Leave 'em wondering what happened."

Tad laughed softly. "I'm ready."

Their voices faded. Nellie, somewhat in shock, was only vaguely aware of receding hoof beats as Tad departed. She softly closed her door and climbed back into bed, crying, her fists clenched, muscles tensed. The shot she'd heard from the ridge—had that been the assassin cutting down Kent? She knew he would've defended himself if he'd had a chance. Only one shot. She couldn't help but suspect Black Rogers. He was capable of gunning down a man from ambush without batting an eye.

Her enraged sobs were muffled in the pillow. She bitterly regretted drawing Kent into this trap that had ended with his death. But the anger and hurt in her breast were directed even more at Grandpa Silas, who seemed glad at this horrible murder. Silas had seen too much hate and death over the years. Vindictiveness was part of his nature. She'd come to look upon him as a gentle, gray-haired grandfather. But, inside, he was still the rebellious Confederate, the vengeful man who retaliated with deadly force against any and all enemies. The blood feud that had simmered for years with the Claytons had been as much his doing as anyone's. Silas had decided, with no proof, that Kent Rasmussen was guilty. Even if he hadn't ordered the ex-Mountie's death, it was only because the Claytons had beat him to the punch. And now her grandfather was laughing because his sworn enemies had done his dirty work for him.

One thing, at least, was very clear to her—she couldn't stay in this house one day longer. She'd pack her few belongings in the morning and go. But go where? Living with any of her uncles was out of the question. Their wives would have none of it. Nellie's reputation had still not recovered from her breach in marrying Johnny Clayton. What a mess! She wiped her tears and lay on her back, staring at the dark ceiling. She should've listened to Kent's advice and gone away to start life anew somewhere else. It wasn't too late. In fact, it was the only course left to her. She'd run out her string here.

As calmness returned, she began to plan. Before

she finally dozed off, after hearing the clock strike two, she'd resolved to flee to Uncle Billy's place. He was neutral. In spite of his eccentricities, he seemed to have a measure of good sense. He'd likely give her shelter for at least a day or two before she moved on. As much as she detested becoming a sneak thief, she had to have some money. There was no safe in the house. What money her grandfather had, he kept in a bank owned by a friend, or in his pockets in the form of greenbacks or gold coin. She could steal his bay saddle horse to make her getaway. But that would cause too much stir. One of her uncles would run her down before she could get five miles away. Her late grandmother's silver service displayed on the sideboard would bring a few dollars if she got to a town, somewhere away from here. But she'd either need a horse, or train fare. She doubted whether Uncle Billy would accept stolen silver in exchange for some of the coin he'd unearthed.

Thus plotting her next move, the tension gradually seeped out of her body and she fell asleep.

The next thing Nellie knew she was awakened by a brisk knock on her door. She pushed back the covers and cracked her eyelids as Grandpa Silas opened the door and shoved his head in.

"Nellie, I'm off on business. Back this afternoon. There will be seven of us for dinner. Plan up the best meal you can think of. I'll leave some money on the hall table. Take the wagon to town and buy what you need. Figure to eat about seven. That's a good girl." His white whiskers stretched in a warm smile, and then he was gone, closing the door behind him.

That hypocritical old man, she thought as she stretched and threw back the sheet to get up. How dare he laugh about the murder of her dear friend, and then project a phony air of paternal care and gentleness?

As she dressed, she thought about confronting him. No. He'd just deny everything. And that would alert him that she was aware of his duplicity and his plans for—for what? She realized she didn't know what nefarious scheme was afoot. Only snatches of conversation had come to her ears—enough to make her suspicious, but not enough to enlighten her. Whatever it was, she wanted no part of it.

But Grandpa Silas had unwittingly played into her hands. By leaving money and telling her to take the wagon to town, he'd given her the means and opportunity to escape. She wouldn't have to go on foot over the ridge to Uncle Billy's, after all.

She was glad her grandfather had left the house early, before she came downstairs. Although he was not usually sensitive to her moods, her demeanor this day would surely have given her away.

Her stomach was a bit queasy, but she forced herself to eat a slice of bread and jam with coffee. Then she found a nearly empty sugar sack, dumped the remaining sugar into a canister, and stuffed the cotton sack with enough food for several meals—bread, dried beef, a side of bacon with its grease soaked muslin wrap still clinging to it, raisins, jars of home-canned plums and tomatoes, tin cans of oysters, dried beans. Even if she didn't eat all this herself, she might be able to trade some of it for things she needed along the way.

Other than food, she'd travel light. She rummaged through the wardrobe in her room and picked out three outfits—one of them a floor-length pale-green dress with matching button shoes and a parasol. At one time in the not too distant past, she'd owned some nice things. But most of it had dwindled down to only a couple of outfits she wore everyday. It didn't take long to pack her small leather grip, folding in most of the underwear she owned, along with two shirtwaists and her only pair of comfortable walking shoes. She put on a cotton riding skirt, her short boots, a blouse, and vest.

Rarely had she used a weapon for anything but target practice, and nearly forgot the tip-up, nickel-plated Smith & Wesson .22 she'd carried on her trip to Canada. Making sure it was loaded, she thrust it under the clothing in her bag, along with a box of fifty cartridges. Best to be prepared for anything. A light, hooded rain cape completed the luggage. Reluctantly she left behind her heavy winter coat. By the time winter set in, she'd be far away—possibly in some warmer climate.

She took her time getting ready in order to allow Grandpa Silas to get wherever he was going. She didn't want to run into him on the road to town. Pausing to fasten the strap on the small bag, she wondered if she should even go to town. Yes, because, if anyone later reported seeing her, they could tell her grandfather she was in Springfield. The main road led southwest, and, even with their old mare pulling the farm wagon, she could be several miles into Oklahoma before Grandpa Silas missed her. She stared out her bedroom window in deep concentration. But what then? They would surely pursue her. The wagon and horse would have to be sold or traded to hide her trail.

By half past eight she was ready. Silas had left $25 on the hall table. Enough to get her started, she thought as she pocketed the bills in her riding skirt and headed for the stable, with the sack of food and her grip. These she stowed in the wagon bed, along with a bag of grain.

The old mare was well past her prime, but still strong enough to pull the weathered wagon to and from town a couple of times a week. She was docile now as Nellie hitched her up.

Nellie climbed to the driver's seat and slapped the reins over the mare's back. Rolling out past the old, two-story house toward the road, she gave the place a lingering look. Likely the last time she'd see it; she didn't anticipate ever coming back. Before all her adult troubles started, she'd had some happy childhood times here, sheltered from the worst of the feud by her mother and grandmother. Looking back on it, she realized they'd done their best to give her as normal an upbringing as was possible under the circumstances.

She turned and looked ahead. That was all behind her now. No more thinking of the past, of hates, of killings and greed and treachery and secret, subversive hooded societies. She had a sudden urge to go West—as far West as possible, perhaps California. Her heart leapt at the thought of a new life, the freedom to do what she wanted, not what she felt obliged to do to satisfy some sense of duty to others.

The road curved through a wooded area, then out into open fields bounded by rail fences. She reached Springfield two hours before noon by the bank clock. Driving casually along the main street, she feared everyone was scrutinizing her, reading her thoughts and intentions. She kept rolling steadily, eyes under her hat brim looking neither left nor right. She half expected to be hailed by friends who wanted to pass the time of day. But no one paid her any mind, and the buildings of Springfield gradually dwindled away. She began to breathe easier, knowing that her fears were only nervous imaginings.

The day wore on and the miles slowly unwound behind her. The road west meandered through stands of heavy hardwood, thick with summer foliage. The dusty track came within a mile of the farmstead of two of Johnny Clayton's uncles. She was apprehensive at first, and wanted to push the tired mare on by quickly. But she resisted the urge when she saw no one. The countryside remained deserted.

In early afternoon she paused to water her horse at a ford that still ran with a tired flow in spite of the dry summer. She put several handfuls of grain in the worn hollow of a flat rock for the mare. This was more work than the old girl had done for some time, and Nellie didn't want to tax the animal's strength. Perhaps the horse could make it another twenty-five miles to Fidelity. If she could reach Joplin or Neosho, she could sell the horse and wagon, then board a train to Oklahoma City, or maybe across Kansas. From there, she had a vague notion of traveling on to New Mexico Territory.

While she sat on a rock, soaking her bare feet in the cool water and munching on bread and jerky, she remembered another picnic, one she and Kent had shared. The thought made the bright day grow dark and her stomach clench. She stopped eating and put the away the remainder of her snack.

She must learn to leave her sad thoughts behind and concentrate on looking ahead. Perhaps she could get a job as a Harvey Girl. She had no saleable skills, except cooking, and the girls who worked for Fred Harvey, serving rail passengers in stops all along the Atchison, Topeka & Santa Fé Railroad, dressed in uniform, were clean and neat and reasonably paid, and were provided a dormitory to live in. Best of all, her chances of meeting an eligible bachelor among the rail passengers were excellent. She'd read there was a large turnover of Harvey House waitresses because they were marrying not long after the expiration of their initial six-month contracts. She believed enough of her youthful good looks remained to get a job as a Harvey Girl. Yet, how could she marry if she was still married to Johnny Clayton? The thought of becoming a bigamist was abhorrent to her. But her marriage existed only on paper now, and she had no desire to stay in Missouri and go through the involved process of obtaining a divorce. When Johnny had become physically abusive to the point that he endangered her life, and had forced her to leave, she felt, in the eyes of God, the union had ceased to exist. From here on, if she ever had occasion to refer to him again, it would be to call him her "ex-husband". In truth, he might well be her *late* husband, if this feud blew up again as she expected it would.

Prospects for her future grew brighter and brighter as she thought about them. She went to wash her hands in the tiny stream. Then she took a gallon crock jug she'd brought, placed a clean handkerchief over the mouth of it, and submerged it on its side in the clearest part of the creek. This water was probably clean enough to drink, but no telling what might be upstream from here. Besides, there were all sorts of tiny organisms in it. And she couldn't afford to be sick now, with no one to care for her.

The jug full, she took a good, long drink, then filled it to the top once more. Putting her things back into the wagon, she reached to gather the reins and climb aboard when a rumble of hoof beats shattered the afternoon stillness.

Before she could put a foot on the wheel hub to climb up, two horsemen rounded a bend and splashed across the creek a few yards from her. It was Johnny Clayton and his cousin, Black Rogers.

A stab of fear went through her and she lunged for her grip in the wagon to get her Smith & Wesson.

"I wouldn't do that, Nellie," Johnny said, leaping to the ground and grabbing her by the arms. She threw herself against the wagon bed, pinning his bandaged hand.

"You bitch!" he yelled, flinging her away and leaning over in agony.

"Let's just shoot her," Rogers said. He slid his Winchester out of its saddle scabbard.

"No, you dumb bastard!" Johnny said through gritted teeth. "We need her." Sweat was popping out on his forehead, but he gingerly took the reins of Nellie's horse with his good hand. "Get aboard," he said to her. "You're going with us."

"Johnny, you and I have had our differences in the past," she said, giving no indication of the butterflies in her stomach. "You got all the money. What do you want with me?"

"Ride behind and trail my horse," Johnny said to Rogers, ignoring her. "I'll drive her in the wagon. Keep us covered, in case she tries something stupid. But don't shoot unless I say to." He motioned for her to board. "It'll be like old times, won't it, Nell?" He gave her a tight grin. "You and me riding together."

She tried again. "Johnny, why don't you just go on about your business, and leave me alone?"

"Nell, you and I will always be soul mates," he replied. The mocking tone had disappeared from his voice.

She glanced at him, wondering: Is that what this

was all about? *Does he really want me back?* Abduction was about the only way he could get her.

"You must have taken a wrong turn somewhere, my dear," he added. "You're nearly eighteen miles west of Springfield."

"Where I go and what I do is none of your damned business!" If she could distract him long enough with conversation and the difficulty of one-handed driving, maybe she could get to her Smith & Wesson. But she'd have to unstrap the grip to get at it. And there was bloody Black Rogers eyeing her, the .45-caliber Winchester across his saddle. She ground her teeth in frustration. She'd been too confident, too sure no one would be after her for several hours until her grandfather finally missed her. She never anticipated Johnny would abduct her. And she had no idea why. She would stall as long as she could but, unless she could somehow discourage him, stalling wouldn't help.

The wagon rattled over the rocks and back onto the road toward Springfield.

She groaned inwardly, knowing she'd been so close to freedom. Now she was a captive once again, in an even worse predicament than if she'd stayed at the Newburn home place.

Chapter Eleven

Kent Rasmussen recognized the peculiar gait of Alex Thorne's mule before it came into view. He let out a breath, slipping his Merwin-Hulbert back into the holster, and stepped out from behind the open door of the shack.

Thorne reined up and dismounted, moving like the much younger man he really was. He hadn't shaved his short white beard, and still wore the overalls, straw hat, and brogans. He tossed a burlap sack of supplies on the table and helped himself to a long drink of water before he spoke.

"Folks in town are pretty stirred up," he said, wiping his mouth with the back of his hand and leaning against the sink. "Word's out that Nellie has been kidnapped by the Claytons."

"What? Why?"

"A lot of opinions about that," Thorne said. "Take your pick. About half the saloon crowd think Johnny is just a hopeless romantic and wants her back as his wife."

"Shit!"

"But the rest think she's being held hostage."

"For what?"

"As their ace-in-the hole in case the Newburns

mount an offensive to get their money back and take revenge for the robbery."

"Not a very honorable way to conduct a feud," Rasmussen said.

"They're no rules when it comes to vengeance. But there's also a strong suspicion in town among experienced feud watchers that the Knights of the Golden Circle are about to make a try for that cold cache."

Rasmussen glanced at him sharply.

"That's where you and I come in," explained Thorne.

"Nellie told me on the train that her grandpa Silas and her cousin are the only ones who know exactly where the treasure's located."

Thorne nodded. "So I've heard. But who really knows? The consistent story is that Silas was one of the knights who helped hide the original stash years ago, during the war. Rumors of vast treasure are usually all smoke. But I'm posing as a treasure hunter, and have actually found the two small stashes I showed you. So I'm convinced a large treasure trove exists. Saw an old report in a Secret Service file in Washington. It was unsigned and vague on details, but indicated some members of a group, then calling itself the Knights of Freedom, transported a large amount of specie to the New Mexico Territory in early Eighteen Sixty-Five. The report was written just after the service was established, and speculated the treasure consisted of the remains of the Confederate Treasury, along with captured Union payrolls and other spoils of war. The report stated this group was headquartered in southern Missouri, and I'm betting these few local knights are the modern remnants of that organization. Subversive societies usually swear their members to secrecy under pain of death. I'm told by folks in town that nearly all those original knights have since died."

"I thought the identity of individual knights was a well-guarded secret."

Thorne chuckled. "In a town this size, there aren't many secrets, especially among the old-timers. The feud and the treasure have provided years of gossip. Speculation is a local hobby. Generally there's a grain of truth hidden under all the bullshit, if you can somehow dig it out. I've listened and listened and bought drinks and acted like I was drunk or bored and heard the same stories in different form at least fifty times in the past six months. When you've been in the undercover business as long as I have, you develop a sense for separating wheat from chaff."

"So, what's your conclusion?"

"Part of this is a hunch based on tidbits I've picked up, but here's what I think. If any of the original knights are still alive, they aren't in any position, by age or circumstances, to mount a try for the cache, because it's that inaccessible. Silas Newburn is the last of the old guard who actually has the knowledge, power, and resources to get it. In case something happens to him before he can recover it, he's drawn up some sort of coded map that indicates the actual location." Thorne paused and went to the still hot stove and poured himself a cup of leftover coffee. Taking a tentative sip of the steaming brew, he continued. "The map could be part of this abduction thing. Nellie might be exchanged for possession of the map, along with an explanation of its codes."

"Have any guesses as to where this cold cache might be?"

"Somewhere many miles from here, if that report was right. The New Mexico-Arizona Territory is mighty big and wild. I worked in and around Tombstone back in 'Eighty-One. Helped break up another secret organization of armed robbers and killers that was being run by an ex-Confederate. This cache could be anywhere."

"That jibes with what Nellie told me on the train," Rasmussen muttered. "She said Silas sent some of her kin to fetch the cache from New Mexico a few years back. They got ambushed by the Claytons before they got the treasure, and nobody wound up with anything but a few dead and wounded men and a continuance of the feud."

"As I see it, Nellie is the keystone that's holding up this whole arch. She's the hostage to keep the Newburns at bay, or she's trading material for possession of the map, or verbal instructions on how to reach the cache. Either way, her life is forfeit if Grandpa Silas doesn't come to terms."

Rasmussen stopped pacing, put a foot up on the chair, leaning his elbows on his knee, stretching the wound in his back that was beginning to itch as it healed. He silently pondered this state of affairs. His only personal experience with the Claytons was with Johnny. His only experience with the Newburns was with Nellie and her grandfather, patriarch of the family. He himself had come into the theater in the third act of this play. Only hearsay told him what'd gone before. Thorne was somewhat more knowledgeable, having lived among these hill folk for months. Yet, the two of them would have to proceed on what they knew, or surmised. He hoped their information was correct. But wasn't that usually the way? If law enforcement were easy, anyone could do it.

The Claytons presently had the upper hand. His and Thorne's only interest in this situation was the location and recovery of the vast treasure—the so-called cold cache that had been hidden for years. By bankrupting the Knights of the Golden Circle, he and Thorne would effectively stop them from trying to split the United States. Easier said than done. The Claytons were far from stupid. And they wanted the treasure as well. They already had a quarter million of it. His face burned with shame, even now, as he recalled how they'd taken it. Not only had they easily stolen the money, but had nearly killed him from ambush in the bargain. It was time to retaliate. In his years with the North-West Mounted Police, he'd hunted men, but usually there was nothing complicated about it. He'd never been in a situation such as this. He straightened up and looked at Thorne.

"It's your call," Rasmussen announced.

"There are several ways we could approach this," Thorne began. "In the guise of Uncle Billy, concerned neighbor, I'll call on Silas and offer my help locating Nellie. He'll, of course, brush me off as irrelevant. But that'll give me a reason to hang around the Newburn place. If I get a sniff about the knights making a move for the treasure trove, you and I can make plans accordingly. The same if there's a hint an all-out war is being planned. I doubt if I'll be able to discover what Silas has in mind about ransoming Nellie with the map, or negotiating her release some other way."

"What do you want me to do in the meantime?"

"Stay here out of sight. As far as anybody knows, you're dead. At least you've disappeared. Anyone who hasn't heard about the shooting, assumes you've gone home. Besides, your wound needs more rest."

In spite of himself, Rasmussen grimaced at the idea of twiddling his thumbs alone at this shack for who knew how long.

"Patience is one thing I've had to learn in this business," Thorne said, noting his involuntary expression. "It didn't come easy for me when I was your age."

Rasmussen knew he was mentally, if not physically, ready for any violent action. He would stay alert and find something to occupy his time. Yet, he knew he'd worry about Nellie. It was her welfare that concerned him more than any treasure, rumored or real.

"OK, I'll stick it out here."

They quickly stowed the staples purchased in town, then ate a lunch of leftover beans and cornbread.

Thorne re-saddled his mule and started over the ridge toward the Newburn house several miles distant.

After the agent's departure, Rasmussen sat at the table, trying to recall his own impression of Johnny Clayton the only time they'd had a chance to talk in the train's dining car the morning after the Chicago depot shooting. That brief encounter and, later, the few venomous words Johnny and Nellie had exchanged during the robbery, were not enough for Rasmussen to form an educated guess as to how Johnny would treat Nellie now that she was his prisoner. Surely her estranged husband would protect her from death, or serious physical harm. But, then, love and hate were but two sides of a single coin. If the wrong side were turned up. . . . Nothing could be assumed when it came to the relations between husband and wife.

He shook his head and got up to distract himself by cleaning up the shack. He tried on the new shirt and pants and boots he'd instructed Thorne to buy for him in town. He was down to only the clothes he'd been wearing for several days, which were badly in need of washing. He heated water on the stove and took a good, soaking bath in the washtub, then washed his old clothes, spreading them on nearby bushes to dry. The refreshing bath and change of clothes did wonders for his outlook. To complete the overhaul, he hunted up a straight razor, a hunk of home-made lye soap, and shaved.

During the rest of that day, he never became so absorbed that he neglected to keep his gun within reach. His senses were on the alert, even when his mind was occupied elsewhere. He couldn't afford to be discovered by anyone now. He'd made too many enemies to reveal his presence—until he was ready.

Due to continuing problems with residuals of frozen toes, he had needed some footgear that was more pliable than the stiff shoes he'd bought in Canada. He'd outlined his foot on a piece of paper, and Thorne had found a pair of boots for him, made of light, supple leather. "You owe me ten dollars extra for those," the older man had said, grinning as he'd tossed the boots to Rasmussen earlier. Now, as he stood up in the new footgear, he knew they were perfect for him. He'd keep them well oiled and maybe they wouldn't shrink the first time they got wet.

He expected Thorne home for supper, but the former Secret Service man didn't appear. Rasmussen became uneasy when 10:00 came and went, then 11:00. Finally he lay down, fully dressed except for his boots and hat, and went to sleep with his revolver by his side.

He awoke at dawn, still alone. He managed to keep himself busy the rest of the day. The older man hadn't said how long he planned to be gone, but Rasmussen resolved to saddle up and go looking for him if he hadn't arrived by the following morning.

Thorne showed that day at sundown. "Supper ready?" he asked, dismounting and striding in, looking well satisfied with himself.

"Where've you been?"

"Tell you over some food."

Fifteen minutes later they sat down to plates of leftover greens and hastily fried ham and potatoes.

"Well?" Rasmussen asked.

"Just like I figured it. Silas's son Tad was there. They were polite enough, but told me to go on home. Brushed me off like the half-cracked, old hermit they think I am. I stalled around a while, pretending to rest my mule, and accepted an offer of something to eat. But it was clear they had things to discuss and went outside to be alone. About then, Otto showed up. . . ."

"Otto?"

"Don't know if that's his first name, or last . . . old man Walter Clayton's hired hand. Acting as sort of an emissary under a flag of truce. I tried my best to hear what he told them, but they were standing out in the yard and I couldn't get too close. When Silas got mad and raised his voice, I managed to get the gist of it. If any of the Claytons are hurt or killed, it'll be an eye for an eye with Nellie. But the courier said Nellie would be returned, unharmed, in exchange for the decoded treasure map."

"I'll bet old man Newburn was fit to be tied."

"You got it." Thorne nodded, cutting a slice of ham. "Thought he was going to have an apoplectic fit on the spot. Called the Claytons everything he could lay his tongue to. 'Goddamned cowards and woman beaters' being some of the milder. Otto jumped on his horse and took off before the old man could pull his gun. Hadn't been for Tad holding back his father, the old man would've gunned down the messenger who brought the bad news."

"That puts the Newburns and the knights in one helluva fix."

"You haven't heard the best part. When I left the Newburn place, I rode into town and did some nosing around. All I found out at first was that Nellie'd been seen driving a wagon in town a couple of mornings before. That was the last anybody recalled seeing her. She hadn't been in the mercantile or the butcher shop or the drugstore. Apparently she wasn't snatched right out of town or somebody would've noticed. I scouted around the countryside the rest of the day, and slept in the woods last night.

"This morning I rode out toward the Clayton farm. From the road, I saw Otto's horse grazing in the pasture. Circled around through the woods until I could view the place from a hill without being seen. Didn't have my field glasses, but thought I recognized the Newburn farm wagon sticking out of a shed. Figured she was probably a prisoner in the farmhouse. It's a good quarter mile from the road, and easily defended, with open pasture all around. Left my mule on the hill and slipped down to the wire fence at the edge of the woods to take a closer look. Sun glinted off a shiny new padlock on a small barn door. Probably a tack room or tool shed. I think that's where the girl's locked up."

"What makes you think so?" Rasmussen asked. "Why wouldn't she be in the house? More humane, and they could keep an eye on her easier there."

"That's what I thought at first. But not so. No real security. A guard would have to be posted around the clock to keep her from running off, and that gets tiresome. They could tie her or chain her, of course, but then she'd have to be loosed every time she had to use a chamber pot or eat. And she'd need at least some exercise. Otto, the hired hand, lives in a tiny house out back. The old patriarch, Walter Clayton, is a widower, and lives there with Johnny, his grandson. Nobody else, according to folks in town. The two of them couldn't come and go freely without pulling guard duty. No. Easier to lock her up in the barn and bring her food and water. She's nothing but chattel. She'll be cared for like a valuable horse . . . tended, but not coddled."

The two men chewed in silence for a long minute.

"Are you thinking what I'm thinking?" Rasmussen finally asked.

"The moon will be almost full tonight," Thorne said.

"We've still got those two rented horses," Rasmussen added.

"How's your back feeling?"

"Couldn't be better," he lied.

"Eat up, then. We'll need our energy."

"Time for a little nap before moonrise."

They grinned at each other.

Rasmussen felt like a twelve-year-old again.

Chapter Twelve

The sun disappeared behind wooded hills.

Rasmussen unloaded his Merwin-Hulbert, removed all the bullets from his belt loops, and carefully wiped off the verdigris from the cartridges casings with an oily rag. While he was reloading, Uncle Billy stepped out of the next room, transformed into Alex Thorne, former Secret Service agent. The overalls had disappeared, along with the brogans. He was attired in tan breeches covered with dark, close-fitting leather chaps. A pale blue shirt stretched across his lean, muscular chest and arms. A black Stetson and polished flat-soled boots completed the outfit. Rasmussen's eyes were drawn to the black gun belt, as Thorne drew his weapon and tested the action of the long-barreled Remington. The old cap-and-ball pistol had been put back on its nail over the door.

"Ready?" Thorne asked.

"Let's go."

Ten minutes later the two men were riding silently down the winding road toward Springfield, Thorne leading on his mule while Rasmussen followed, trailing the saddled spare horse. Every minute or so they could glimpse the rising moon—a huge orange ball—through breaks in the trees.

The Clayton farm was ten miles beyond town, Thorne estimated, so they rode slowly to save the animals and to kill time, hoping everyone would be asleep before they arrived.

Two hours later the moon, high overhead, was a silver disk, bathing the landscape in an eerie light and etching sharp, black shadows.

There was no wind to mask the sounds of their movements. But the hoof beats were muffled in the deep grass alongside the dirt track where they rode to keep from stirring up the powdery dust. The road was deserted. Under the darkness of overhanging trees, Rasmussen had to rely on the sounds of Thorne ahead of him.

It seemed an eternity before they passed north of town and covered another ten miles. Thorne finally reined up his mule in chest-high weeds. He pointed. Across a wire fence in front of them, a split log barn with high gables hunkered in the middle of a pasture. On the near side, where the moonlight struck it fully, small gaps were visible between the unchinked logs. It looked old, but stoutly built. Something about it seemed odd, though. Then Rasmussen realized it was blackened, as if it'd survived a fire, more than just the weathering of age.

"Looks like it's used to smoke-cure tobacco," he said in an undertone.

Thorne nodded, his mind apparently elsewhere. "The padlocked door is on the end there," he said, pointing.

Rasmussen felt a bit queasy, and not only because of the miasma emanating from the hog pens just beyond the barn. This place was too wide open. With the bright moonlight, they might as well make an assault on the barn in broad daylight. A good 100 yards of pasture stretched between the weed-choked fence row and the barn, and another 100 upslope to the two-story white farmhouse. What was worse for their purpose, a light still illuminated one of the upstairs windows.

They'd be better advised to wait for a cloudy or stormy might, or at least until there was no moon. From the upper floor of that house, anyone with a pair of field glasses could spot a pack rat crossing that moonlit field. But they couldn't risk waiting for a better opportunity. Silas Newburn could make his move at any time, and it wasn't likely he'd give up the location of the treasure to secure Nellie's release. It was possible—even likely—that the Knights of the Golden Circle were in session at this very hour, plotting strategy. Rasmussen's instincts, honed during years as a Mounted Policeman, cried out against this raid. The odds weren't right. But they had to try, and they had to try tonight.

The two men sat motionlessly in their saddles, contemplating the layout. If there were any cattle on the place, they were in another pasture. Except for the distinctive stink from the hog pens fouling the fresh air, it was a nostalgic scene—the barn posing serenely in the middle of a moonlit pasture, awaiting the talent of some artist to reproduce it on canvas.

Rasmussen would have felt better about this scheme if he were even certain Nellie was imprisoned there. For all he knew, they might be burglarizing an empty barn, or one being used to store plows and harrows and old harness.

Thorne motioned and led the way slowly toward

the cover of the woods. They made their way up-hill through the woods, parallel to the fenced property, then dismounted in the inky shadows and tethered the animals to saplings.

"Slide along the fence till we're opposite this end of the barn, then we won't have so much open space to cross," Thorne whispered. He held up a short, iron tool. "I'll pry off the hasp. No telling what kind of shape the girl's in. Might even be asleep. Just snatch her up between us and run like hell for the woods."

Rasmussen was irritated to see the fence consisted of four strands of barbed wire, strung tightly between iron posts. "Better take care of this first. We didn't bring any wire cutters."

They each grabbed a thin post, rocked it back and forth in unison until loosened enough to push a section of the fence nearly flat to the ground. *"Ow!"* Even with gloves protecting his hands and wrists, the steel barbs found a way to hook Rasmussen's shirt sleeve and rake his forearm. They stood on the flattened fence, not having a rock handy to weight it down. Rasmussen drew a deep breath. Barbed wire was one of the cruelest, and least necessary, inventions of mankind. In his experience, the only herding animal that couldn't be held by ordinary wire or wooden fencing was the buffalo. Their nature was to drift north and south on open range, following the seasons of grass.

"We'll just have to chance it that nobody's watching," Thorne said. "Take it slow and easy to the barn. Move a few yards, stop, then repeat. I'll go first, you come after and cover me."

Rasmussen grunted his assent, recalling the way a bullet from the unseen rifleman had felt hitting his back. "You didn't see anything of a guard?"

"Not unless somebody's watching from the house. Just as easy to stand guard from there on a bright night like this. We'll have to chance it."

Rasmussen drew his gun, worked the action, then eased the hammer down.

"Don't shoot unless absolutely necessary," Thorne said.

"Right." His partner didn't know he'd been trained in restraint. The North-West Mounted Police had always maintained a shoot last policy, mostly because they were nearly always outnumbered and outgunned. Therefore, they made it a practice to resolve conflict and apprehend criminals with a firm, but fair, approach, using the sight of the uniform backed by the potential force of Her Majesty's government. It didn't always work.

Thorne stepped cautiously into the open and moved across the open pasture, freezing in position every few yards. When he was halfway there, Rasmussen followed, making for the shaded side of the barn. He didn't exert himself, but was breathing rapidly by the time he reached the depth of shadows against the wall. Gazing at the house, he realized it would be nearly impossible to see out from the inside of the lighted room on the second floor. More likely, if anyone were watching, it would be from the porch or a darkened window.

Every minute seemed to drag like fifteen. He stood motionlessly, fingering his holstered gun. What was Thorne doing? He could hear *clanking* and *scraping* as his partner worked the crowbar.

Finally the silhouette of Thorne's hat appeared around the corner. "Can't pry it off," he whispered. "Feels like it's bolted all the way through."

"Shit!"

"I'll have to shoot it off. Be ready."

Rasmussen came to the corner and held his breath as Thorne pointed his Remington at the shiny padlock, then turned his face away to avoid any splatter of metal.

BOOM! BOOM!

The serene night was shattered by the explosions. Flame lanced from the barrel, the second shot spinning the big lock away.

"Nellie!" Thorne yelled.

A throaty roar. A furry projectile hurtled from the black opening.

"Aaagghh!" Thorne stumbled and fell backward. The dog went over him and sprang for Rasmussen's throat.

With lightning reflexes, Rasmussen jerked his head to the left, and felt the hot snap of fangs by his ear. But the dog's big body slammed into his right chest, spinning him down. He rolled over, did a backward somersault, and came to his feet, reaching for his gun. It was gone.

The animal hit the ground off balance, staggered, regained his balance, and pivoted to go for his quarry again. Instantly a vision was burned into Rasmussen's retina—black hair bristling on the back of an Alsatian bigger than a wolf, exposed fangs gleaming in the moonlight. Rasmussen dodged and sprinted toward the first cover he saw—the slats of the hog pen, ten yards away. Two steps upslope and he stumbled in the deep grass, rolling onto his back as the brute leaped for him again. Rasmussen flexed his knees, caught the leaping animal in the belly with both boots, and thrust his legs upward, propelling the dog in an arc above his head, and over the board fence behind him where the animal landed on his back among the resting hogs in the pen.

Ignoring the pandemonium of grunting, squealing, and growling, Rasmussen scrambled to his feet, grabbed his hat, and dashed for the barn where Thorne was still on his hands and knees.

"Here's your gun."

Rasmussen caught the nickel-plated weapon that flashed through the moonlight. "Where is she?" Rasmussen jumped for the open door. "Nellie! Nellie!" he shouted, feeling his way into the inky blackness, hands in front of him, holding his gun. "If you're in here, yell or kick or bang on something, so I can find you!" He stumbled into a piece of machinery and gashed his arm on sharp metal. His eyes quickly grew accustomed to the dimness. He could distinguish large objects in the slits of moonlight filtering through the cracks in the log wall. There was no sign of anyone, whether tied up, unconscious, or asleep.

Thorne thrust his head in. "Let's get out of here. It was a trap!" he rasped.

Rasmussen stumbled outside, and the two men ran for the fence.

Gunfire roared from the house, drowning the snarling, squealing battle in the hog pen. Muzzle flashes erupted from the porch. A bullet *zipped* into the grass ahead of Rasmussen. He leaned down and ran, dodging from one side to the other. Shooting downslope at moving targets in uncertain light at a distance of more than 100 yards didn't make for accuracy. But there was always the element of luck. He hoped they were using handguns instead of rifles.

The fence row at the edge of the woods didn't

seem any closer. The fusillade increased, and he felt the tug of a bullet passing through his shirt sleeve.

Suddenly Thorne went down in front, nearly tripping him. Rasmussen hooked the smaller man under one arm and began dragging him. Sweat was streaming from his face; his lungs began to burn with the effort. A surge of adrenaline drove him on. A bullet snatched off his hat, and he crouched even lower, pulling his burden with renewed effort.

By the time they reached the fence and woods, they were nearly hidden from the house by a swell of ground. The gunfire slacked off.

"I'm all right," Thorne gasped, pulling free and tottering to his feet. "Bullet tore off my boot heel. Numbed my foot."

Rasmussen flattened the barbed wire and helped his partner cross. They began the slog uphill to their mounts. A few minutes later they were riding hard toward the road, safely away.

When the first two shots banged out, Walter Clayton started up from a doze, grabbed his revolver from the gun belt on a chair, and extinguished the lamp. Rolling silently out of bed, he edged to the open window and pulled back the curtain. A struggle near the barn.

Johnny's footsteps *thudded* past his door and went pounding down the stairs.

Walter heard a vicious snarling, then squeals and grunts, but the hog pen was hidden in the deep shadow of the barn. His hired hand, Otto, must be shooting at a coyote or wolf trying to snatch one of the piglets, he thought. He'd never known predators to be that bold in summer when small game was plentiful. Then he noted the door at the end of the barn standing open. A figure dodged inside and someone yelled Nellie's name. Walter suddenly knew his trap had been sprung. Two men sprinted away from the barn and across the moonlit expanse of pasture. Gunfire blasted from the porch below.

"Come on . . . come on!" he urged the other gunmen under his breath.

But neither of the running men fell at first. The roar of shots from Johnny and Otto became incessant. Then, near the shelter of woods, the leading figure went down.

"Got him!" Walter breathed, clenching his .44.

The second man stooped to help, and the fire from below slackened.

"Shoot! Shoot, you ninnies, while they're not moving!" Walter hissed. But then he realized the fleeing men were probably hidden from view to the shooters on the porch below. He thumbed back the hammer of his Colt, hunkered down, and rested his arm on the open window sill. The Colt bucked and roared, plucking the hat off one man's head. "Damn!" He was shooting high. He lowered his aim and fired again. He'd overcorrected. He fired a third time, but the figures were moving again. Before he could draw a bead, they disappeared into the black shadows of the treeline.

"Go after them!" Walter roared out the window.

He watched his grandson and the hired hand dash down into the yard, one with a rifle and one carrying a revolver. They ran down the grassy slope toward the spot where the two men had vanished. But then, apparently realizing they could be ambushed in the darkness, they came to a halt and fired several shots into the woods. For a few seconds they stood talking. Then Johnny picked up the hat that had been shot off. The pair retreated slowly toward the house, glancing back over their shoulders.

Walter Clayton shoved his gun back into its holster, relit the lamp, and pulled off his nightshirt. He struggled into a pair of pants. Damned things were getting too tight. Looking into the washstand mirror he smoothed his remaining strands of hair, then shrugged into a loose shirt that disguised his rotund build. By this time, he heard Johnny and Otto talking in the hallway below and padded, barefooted, downstairs.

"How in hell did you two miss them?" he demanded. "I guess if you want something done, you have to do it yourself."

Johnny made his bandaged hand more conspicuous, as if that were an excuse for faulty marksmanship.

"Go check on Nellie," Walter ordered.

Otto disappeared toward the fruit cellar, and Walter turned to Johnny.

"I laid that trap so we could bag us a Newburn or two, but you let 'em slip away," he said.

"I heard you shooting, too," Johnny said defensively.

"With a Colt. And without my glasses," the old man said, his anger beginning to cool as he reached for the hat his grandson still held. "Lemme see that. We might be able to trace this back to the owner." He held it to the moonlight streaming through the window. "*Hmmm.* Looks new." He went to the marble-top table near the front window and, taking a match from a holder, struck it to the coal-oil lamp, turning it up to illuminate the room. "Hardly been worn. No name or initials. Reckon if it was just bought, we can check the mercantile or the men's haberdashery in town. Some cheap brand . . . not a Stetson." He put his finger through one of the two bullet holes in the crown. "That was my shot," he said with a touch of pride. "Reckon I ain't quite lost it yet."

Otto returned. "She's still there, sleeping," he reported. "Down in that cellar, she likely never heard the shooting."

Walter nodded. "We've still got our hole card." He turned to Johnny. "Go see what all that damned ruckus was with the hogs," he said. "Sounded like the dog got into the pen. Hope to hell he or the sow didn't kill each other." He turned toward the stairs. "Otto, pour me a shot of whiskey so I can go back to sleep. In the morning, I'll take this hat to town, and find out who one of our night visitors was."

Chapter Thirteen

The ride to Thorne's shack seemed endless. To frustrate pursuit, Rasmussen and Thorne detoured south of Springfield, then rode cross-country, taking advantage of the waning moonlight and Thorne's knowledge of the terrain. Coming back onto the main road east from town, they halted to rest the horses and await anyone following.

A quarter hour later, Thorne rose stiffly from the ground. "Nobody's coming. They're too savvy to go chasing armed men in the dark."

"Reckon so," Rasmussen said as they retrieved their horses and mule from the edge of the trees and remounted. "But I have a quivering sensation between my shoulder blades, like someone's drawing a bead on me."

Thorne chuckled. "Probably your wound."

The men rode slowly east, with Rasmussen keeping an eye on their back trail.

"The Claytons know this country a lot better than I do," Thorne said. "If they saddled up right away, they could've gotten around us and be waiting up ahead."

"Maybe so . . . if they knew we were going east."

"If we'd headed west, we would've passed right by

that pasture and barn again," Thorne said. "I don't think anyone's coming. But look sharp, anyway."

They eventually reached Thorne's shack without incident, having met no one on the road. By Thorne's estimate, it was close to three o'clock in the morning. After putting up the animals with a rub-down and some grain, Thorne cleaned the gash on Rasmussen's forearm.

"Gouged it on a hay rake," Rasmussen said.

"Pull off that shirt. The back of it's bloody, too. Guess you busted open your wound."

"Ruined a new shirt."

"It'll wash." Thorne tossed it into a bucket. Then he rubbed salve on both wounds.

Rasmussen slipped into his old shirt while Thorne took off his boots and used a stick of stove wood to hammer the scarred boot heel back into place. His heel was bruised and sore, but otherwise OK.

"We were damned lucky," Thorne remarked, pulling his sock back on. "My blunder could've cost us our lives."

No excuses, no evading responsibility. Rasmussen appreciated a plain-spoken professional.

"I misjudged the situation. Somebody put that big, shiny new padlock on the barn, hoping a fool like me, or one of the New-burns, would figure Nellie was inside. Sprung the trap with a vicious dog."

"Lucky that hog pen was close," Rasmussen said, still hearing the snap of the teeth next to his ear, "or the Claytons wouldn't have needed their guns."

"When that dog came flying out the door, I thought it was a wolf," Thorne said.

"Not likely they'd have a wolf on the place," Rasmussen remarked.

"I don't know about that . . . those Claytons are a strange bunch."

"That Alsatian was bigger than any wolf I ever saw in Canada or Minnesota," Rasmussen said, lowering himself wearily onto a chair by the table.

"Wonder why that dog didn't raise a ruckus while I was trying to rip off the hasp?"

"Maybe thought it was his owner coming to feed him," Rasmussen said. "But, then, some guard dogs are trained to attack without warning. All bite and no bark." He stretched his weary muscles. He suddenly missed his brown felt hat. "A bullet took that new hat right off my head when we were making a run for it."

Thorne looked up sharply. "Did you put your name or initials in it?'

"No marks at all."

"Good. You can bet they'll find it and try to trace the owner. Even if they do, we'll still have a little time." Thorne went to the screen door and stepped outside, looking and listening for a minute. "All quiet," he said, returning.

"For how long?"

"I'd say at least until late tomorrow."

"I'll stand first watch until daylight," Rasmussen said, noting the drawn look on the older man's face. "I'm too keyed up to sleep right now anyway, and these wounds are aching." he added when Thorne opened his mouth to object. He picked up Thorne's shotgun and broke it open to check the loads. "You know, the Claytons could have set a couple of bear traps in that dark barn."

"The dog was quicker and surer," Thorne said. "These families play rough. Nothing too low-down."

"I'd always read that feuding clans were honorable and brave, would challenge an enemy straight up."

"Only in fiction," Thorne said, yawning. "Nobody would mistake the Newburns and Claytons for the Montagues and Capulets." He went into the bedroom and stretched out on his stomach, fully dressed except for his boots. Within two minutes, he was softly snoring.

Rasmussen sat in a straight chair, facing the screen door, shotgun across his lap. Crickets *chirping*, a bullfrog's deep-throated *croaking* from somewhere—all peaceful sounds of the night, completely different from hours before, and miles away.

Every fifteen or twenty minutes, he walked outside to keep himself awake. He'd always hated night watches and guard duty when his police patrol was in the field near hostile Indians or camped near outlaw quarry. As always, this night seemed to stand still and he suffered the agony of fighting the weariness that dragged at his limbs and eyelids.

He checked the stable, then came back inside, turned the lamp lower, and looked in on Thorne. Asleep, and without the vitality energizing his face, the former Secret Service agent looked his age. He was not an old man by normal standards—not nearly as antiquated as he pretended to be in the guise of Uncle Billy, eccentric hermit. Early fifties, Rasmussen guessed—at least old enough to be retired from a hazardous federal career. Thorne's stamina might not be what it had been, but his experience more than made up for that. True, he'd miscalculated Nellie's location. But Thorne struck him as the type who admitted mistakes, learned from them, and moved on without recriminations. He made the best decisions he could, based on what he knew, or guessed. If those decisions proved wrong, then he'd back up and attack from another direction. With luck, he would be right more often than wrong. The problem was, in this line of work, a single error of judgment could be fatal.

He resumed his post on the chair. In spite of himself, his chin sank on his chest and he began to dream. He jerked awake with a hand on his shoulder.

"Kent, take it easy. It's me," Thorne's voice reassured him.

"Huh?" Rasmussen was still groggy. "I could be cashiered for sleeping on watch," he said, embarrassed, stumbling to his feet, one leg partially asleep.

Thorne grinned. "As I recall, you've already cashiered yourself out of the Mounted Police."

Rasmussen handed over the shotgun without replying and headed for the adjacent bedroom. He sank down on the rumpled bed and was asleep before he knew it.

He awoke to the aroma of fresh coffee and frying bacon. The sun was high and Thorne had prepared lunch. They sat down and did the meager meal justice.

"Where do we go from here?" Rasmussen asked, deferring to the more experienced lawman. "Are we the hunters or the hunted?"

Thorne grinned. "Been giving that some thought. I believe our best bet is to lie low and see what Silas Newburn does. As I figure it, he has to go after Nellie, or the Claytons, or the gold. He can't allow the *status quo* to exist for more than a day or so. He'll get the blame for our raid last night and that'll stir him up even more. The Claytons have challenged him with the robbery and now kidnapping his granddaughter as a hostage. It's like cornering a badger. We're going to see some action pretty quick."

Rasmussen drained his coffee cup and wiped his mouth. "This is a mighty strange business. I don't like not being in control."

"What do you suggest?" Thorne asked, leaning back and crossing his legs.

"I can't stand inaction. Let's raid the Clayton place. They won't expect us a second time."

"Yes, they would. We'd probably get Nellie killed, since we've already put them on the alert with that business last night. You're forgetting that most folks around here think you're dead. If you reveal yourself, you might not be as lucky next time. The Claytons sent Black Rogers to kill you. And Silas suspects you of complicity in the robbery. He'd just as soon see you permanently out of the picture as well. You're *persona non grata* to both sides."

"Damn," Rasmussen breathed softly. "We've got to do something."

Thorne rose and stretched. "Sit tight here and keep a sharp look-out. I'll ride to town and see if I can pick up any rumors. Won't be long. Back before sundown."

Nellie Newburn thumped her fists on the underside of the wooden cellar door. She had to get out and move around, see daylight, breathe fresh air. She had a coal-oil lamp to illuminate her dirt-walled prison. Even though it was turned very low, it still gave off an offensive odor that fouled the stale air.

She'd tried to keep track of when it was day or night, but had grown disoriented. After Johnny had escorted her to the outhouse several times, he caught on to her ploy for temporary freedom and gave her a white porcelain slop jar with lid, denying further releases from the hole. The slop jar further deteriorated the air quality. She was dirty, tired, thirsty, and living like a mole. Her entreaties to Johnny fell on deaf ears. But she had to try again.

Had anyone heard her pounding on the trap door? Most of the hand-dug dirt cellar was beneath the side yard of the house. Only the four wooden steps were inside the edge of the wall so the cellar door could open through the plank floor of the living room.

Finally she heard the iron ring *clank* and the door was yanked upward and thrown back. Otto stood there, gun drawn.

"Whaddya want?"

She hesitated, blinking at the bright daylight. What could she say? That she wanted out? He knew that. She was a prisoner. She quickly thought of some plausible excuse. "Can you empty my slop jar?"

"Is it full?"

"No, but. . . ."

"Call me when it is."

"I want to talk to Johnny."

"He ain't here."

"Walter, then."

"They're both gone to town. I'm in charge."

She stepped up and thrust her head above the floor. Morning light. She tried a desperate ploy. "I haven't had a bath since I've been here. And I'm really dirty down in this hole." She hesitated. "I'm unarmed and can't do anything." She gave him an ingratiating smile. "Would you be so kind as to heat up some water for a bath, while we're both here alone?"

Holstering his gun, the lean man shook his head. "Johnny'd skin me alive. If he didn't, Mister Clayton would fire me."

"Oh, please. . . ." She let her voice convey all the misery and helplessness she felt. "What can it hurt? I'll be quick." She dropped her eyes and made to blush. "I'll even let you watch, if you want."

She looked up and saw his prominent Adam's apple bob up and down as he glanced out the window. "I can't. Too risky. They might come back any time."

"How long they been gone?" She grew bolder and leaned both elbows and her breasts over the edge of the floor-level door.

His gaze took in her figure under the grimy blouse. He paced to the window and looked toward the road. "Uh . . .'bout an hour."

"Then, don't worry. They probably won't be back till after lunchtime."

He came toward her. "OK, but this has got to be quick." He dragged the tin bathtub from under the sink in the kitchen and set it near the stove.

She watched as he pumped four buckets of water at the sink, then poured them into the tub, slopping water on the hardwood floor in his haste. He stoked up the fire and set a pot of water on to heat.

Catching his eye, she gave him a bold look and began unbuttoning her blouse.

He licked his lips and swallowed as he worked, fear and desire in his eyes. "Takin' a big chance," he said, splashing another bucket of water into the tin tub.

The water on the stove began to steam, and she slipped off her top and dropped it on the floor. Pointed breasts bouncing, she walked closer as he poured in the hot water to temper the bath. She pretended not to notice him gaping at her as she unbuttoned her riding skirt and let it fall, along with her pantaloons, and stood naked before him. He seemed mesmerized by the sight. Now for the *coup de grâce.*

"You know, Otto, you're a good-looking man. Johnny never treated me like a real woman. I'll bet you would."

"Yeah . . . yeah!" He seemed to have trouble getting his breath. Edging toward her, he put out a calloused hand to touch her left breast.

"Not yet," she said, stepping back. "Let me take a quick bath first. We have plenty of time." She lifted a leg and tested the water daintily with one foot. "Might be good if you cleaned up a little, too. Maybe scrape those whiskers off."

He seemed to wake up suddenly. "No, no. They'd wonder why I was shaving in the middle of the week."

"Then rinse off under the pump. You smell sweaty." She wrinkled her nose.

He stripped off his shirt and let it hang from his belt while he began working the pump handle on the edge of the sink. He thrust his head under the gushing water, continuing to pump with one hand as the water streamed over his tangled black hair.

While his eyes were closed and the pump *clanking*, she slipped to the woodbox, gripped a heavy stick of split oak, and came up behind him. Holding her breath, she took careful aim and struck a solid blow just above his right ear. He fell as if he'd been tackled at the knees, rolled limply onto his back, and lay still. She snatched the .38 Smith & Wesson from his holster and drew back, wary, lest he wake up. But the pale, wet face didn't move, and she had a sudden qualm. Had she hit him too hard, perhaps killed him? She bent down and felt his throat for a pulse. It was steady. She fished in his pockets, found a ratty billfold, and extracted the $11 it contained.

Still naked, she grabbed him by one foot and dragged him to the open cellar door and tumbled him down the four steps. She tilted the heavy door and let it fall into place.

Breathing quickly with fear and excitement, she dressed again, regretting she had no time to enjoy a good bath. Thrusting the stolen gun under the waistband of her skirt, she ran out the back door. At the stable, the only saddle horse left was Otto's. She snatched the bridle off a nail and slipped it over the horse's head, buckling it. Then she tied the reins to a stall post while she threw on the saddle blanket, smoothing it into place. Within another minute she had the gelding saddled and led him outside. All clear. No one on the road. She mounted, kicking the horse into a run out the gate, then turned west. This animal was no endurance runner, and could never carry her as far or as fast as she wanted to go.

The horse quickly worked up a lather, his withers heaving. Not wanting to tire him, she slowed to a walk for a mile. Thank God, no one was on the road. She urged him to a trot him for two more miles, until she sensed him laboring again.

A train whistle sounded off to her right. A half minute later, it wailed again—a little closer. Her heart leaped. It was the daily westbound express from Springfield. That was her escape! The train was no more than a mile away, blowing for a crossing. She turned off the road and started through the woods to intersect the tracks. On a tired horse, she had no hope of catching the train if it was moving at full speed. She was roughly thirty miles west of town by now, and the steam locomotives usually stopped at a water tank not far from here. Maybe that would allow her just enough time.

She heard the wail of the steam whistle no more, but pushed her horse as fast as she dared through the rough undergrowth, over rotting logs, around deadfalls and thickets of blackberry bushes. Luckily she encountered no wire fences. Unlike most of the Ozarks, the terrain here was reasonably level.

Could she intercept the train? Surely she deserved a break. Somehow, she must get aboard, whether it was a passenger or freight. The railroad was the quickest and surest way out of this part of the country. It was about the right time for the express that left Springfield every day at 10:50.

Through the trees ahead, she glimpsed a stationary train, and breathed a prayer of thanks. Reining up just where the woods had been cleared for the right of way, she saw the locomotive panting quietly beneath a gushing water spout. She dismounted and slapped the horse on the rump. "Hyah! Git!" The horse lunged away. He'd find his way back to the stable.

Where was the conductor? She'd go aboard and buy a ticket for as far as $8 would take her. The remainder of the $11 would be saved to buy food. Dirty, and with no luggage, a pistol in the waistband of her riding skirt, he'd look askance at her, but what the hell . . . ? If she encountered any local people, it was likely they'd know of the kidnapping. Would they try to interfere with her, or would they welcome her back? Time to find out.

She stepped out, waded through the weeds, and climbed up the sloping rail bed. The counterbalanced water spout was being swung upward. They were about to get under way.

Behind the mogul locomotive and tender was hitched the baggage car, then the Pullman, followed by a dining car, two day coaches, and the caboose.

Nellie walked along the roadbed to the first day coach. The train jerked into motion as she grabbed the handrail and jumped aboard.

Apparently the conductor had seen her approaching, and now accosted her as she mounted the iron steps to the platform at the end of the car.

"You got a ticket?"

She felt his eyes taking in her grubby appearance. "I want to buy one," she answered quickly, pulling the folded bills from the pocket of her skirt.

"Where to?"

"How far will eight dollars take me?"

He appeared to be making mental calculations. "Sapulpa . . . a little way beyond Tulsa in the Territory."

"Is that all?" Her stomach fell.

"When we get on down into the Nations, maybe we could work out some other arrangement so you can go farther," he said.

She pretended not to see his knowing smile.

"How much is this worth?" she asked, pulling Otto's .38 revolver.

He looked startled until she turned it, butt first, to him.

"Company can't take goods in trade for tickets," he said. "But you and I might make some arrangement between ourselves. I could put in the cash for you. How far you want to go?"

She thought quickly. "New Mexico."

"Santa Fé?"

"Yes."

He took the $8, and pulled out a book of tickets,

ruffling through them until he found one he wanted. He wrote something on it in pencil, punched both ends, tore it in two, and gave her half. "Here's a one-way ticket to Sapulpa." His curiosity was not yet satisfied. "No luggage? No handbag?"

"This was an emergency."

"Appears so." He went back inside and she followed, hesitating at the door to scan the faces of the passengers. They were all strangers to her. She sighed with relief for the first time in several days, and took the first empty seat next to a window.

She would not have been so relaxed had she entered the Pullman, two cars ahead.

Chapter Fourteen

"You recognize this hat?" Walter Clayton held out the brown felt headpiece for the clerk in his mercantile to examine.

"Can't say as I do." He took it and looked inside at the sweatband. "We don't carry this brand." He looked at the frowning face of his big boss, the owner of a third of the businesses on this street. "It's not one we usually stock. It might've been part of a special shipment we ordered for a spring sale. But I can't say for certain it's one we handled. Exeter is a common brand. As you know, sort of low-end quality."

"When did we stop marking every piece of our merchandise with my initial?" Walter demanded.

The clerk made a show of looking inside again. "We only ink our regular stock with your tiny C, sir," he said.

"So you don't know for a fact that our store handled this particular hat?"

"Well . . . it looks like one we might've sold," the clerk hedged. "Except, of course, for the hole in it." He grinned.

Walter Clayton was in no mood for jokes. "You were on duty every working day for the past two or three weeks?"

"Yes, sir. Every day that we were open."

"By yourself?"

"Most of the time."

"And you don't remember selling a hat identical to this one in that time . . . since the sale last spring?

"Well . . . it's hard to recall every piece of merchandise I've sold. . . ."

"Think, man!" Walter thundered.

The clerk jumped.

"This hat looks new," Walter went on, noting the blank look on the clerk's face. "Unless the owner put it away somewhere and didn't wear it, it had to have been bought within the last week or so."

"Uh . . . there was that old hermit in here yesterday . . . what's his name? I don't recall."

"I know who you mean. Go on."

"Well, he bought a few things . . . dried beans and such, a shirt and our best pair of leather boots. I wondered at the time how he had enough to pay eighteen dollars for them. But it's rumored he's found some buried coins in. . . ."

"Never mind all that!" Walter snapped. "What about him?"

"Besides some staples and a shirt and pants and boots, he bought a hat like that. Now as I think on it, it was identical. I remember, 'cause he tried it on first and it came down over his ears. Looked like a clown." He grinned at the recollection. "Thought he'd pick out another one, but he said that one was perfect, even though it was 'way too big for him."

Walter looked at the size—7¾ What if the old hermit wasn't buying the hat for himself? For whom, then? Did one of the Newburns have a head that big? But why would the recluse be shopping for them? It didn't make sense.

* * *

"He goes by the name Uncle Billy," Johnny informed his grandfather when Walter put the question to him outside on the street a half hour later.

"What do you know about him?"

"Nothing much. Hear tell he came here a few months ago to hunt for treasure."

"Oh?"

"The old man's a little cracked," Johnny said. "Nobody pays him any mind. I see him in town now and again."

"Maybe he's half cracked," Walter said, thrusting a finger through one of the bullet holes in the felt, "but somebody wearing this hat he bought was at our place last night. And I mean to find out who it was."

"Let's take a ride out to see him. His shack is a few miles east of town."

Walter hesitated. Did he really want to make that ride right now? He hated to admit it, but his well-padded posterior hadn't protected him from feeling sore as a result of the ten-mile ride into town from his farm. He should have brought the buggy, but didn't want to let his grandson think he wasn't still up to forking a frisky Quarter horse when there was work to be done. As a diversion from responding to the suggestion, he said: "I thought you were going to have the doc look at your hand."

"I did. That's where I've been for the last hour. There were three ahead of me in his office." He grimaced. "This town is gettin' too damned big. People everywhere. Have to wait to see the doc. Before you know it, he'll get so busy, he won't make house calls any more. Patients will. . . ."

"What did he say?" Walter cut in.

"My hand's healing pretty well. He took the bandage off, and said I should wear a big glove for another week or two to protect it."

"At least that's good news. And the bastard who shot you's been plowed under, so that score is settled."

"Maybe it is," Johnny said, holding up the hand. The thumb was curled in toward the palm and the barely-healed flesh still bore a bluish cast.

"What do you mean . . . maybe?"

"Doc says I might never get back the full use of this hand. Something about the tendon being damaged. He doubts surgery would help."

"Rasmussen . . . that son-of-a-bitch!" Walter spat. "Wish he was standing here right now so I could have the pleasure of putting out his lights myself."

"It's over, Grandpa. No need gettin' riled at him. The man's dead. Black Rogers took care of him."

"Rogers never found the body," Walter said, pursing his lips.

Johnny dismissed this with a shake of his head. "You know these hills. He was probably dragged off by coyotes or mountain lions, and eaten. Whatever varmints got him must 'a' spooked his horses, too, 'cause Rogers didn't find them, either."

Walter let it go. "Nobody hurts me or mine and gets away with it," he said. "If Rasmussen's dead, so be it. So's that Newburn who shot you in the knee back when you ran off with Nellie." He ground his teeth, staring down the street toward the depot where the daily westbound express was *clanging* and puffing to a stop. But his mind was filled with hate at everything and everyone connected with the Newburns. They'd been the bane of his existence, and he wouldn't be satisfied until every last one of them, from the oldest to the youngest, was under the sod, or being plucked by the buzzards and crows. He'd damned sure put a few of them down himself, he thought with grim satisfaction.

This brought to mind his oldest, most formidable enemy, Silas Newburn. But he had that skinny old bastard by the short, white whiskers for sure, now. If Silas didn't come through with the location of the treasure, his granddaughter Nellie would be added to the list of the late Newburns. Walter didn't care if she was a female. Like scorpions, they were often more dangerous than the males.

"Do you want to ride out there or not?"

Walter was jolted out of his reverie by Johnny's question.

"Out where?"

"To find that Uncle Billy character."

Walter drew a deep breath. "I'm gonna get me a haircut and shave first. Then something to eat. No rush. He's not going any place."

"If he raided our place last night, he might be on the run already," Johnny said, a look of urgency on his face.

"I doubt if that old hermit was one of the raiders. But he very likely knows who was. Probably has no idea we're after him, so he has no reason to run. We can afford to take our time."

He hitched up his pants that were sagging under the unaccustomed weight of his gun belt. He shouldn't wear his hardware when he had on suspenders. "The express just pulled in. While I'm at the barber, run down to the depot and get me a copy of the Saint Louis Post-Dispatch before they're all sold."

Walter Clayton had always had a fondness for barbershops. A modest drinker himself, he preferred them to saloons. There were no loud-mouth or sick drunks, no raucous laughter or shouting or music, no perfumed whores to wheedle money from a man who wanted only to relax with a pint. While a man awaited a haircut or refreshing shave, he could discuss anything and everything—from the vicissitudes of women to horse racing or boxing, crops to politics. And there were always the latest jokes.

Sam had already trimmed the fringe of hair around Clayton's ears and neck and had wrapped his face in a steamy towel to soften his whiskers. Tilted back in the chair, Walter was nearly dozing when Sam carefully removed the towel and began to apply hot lather with the brush. Walter opened his eyes in time to glance at a man walking in the door.

"Sam, hand me my specs."

"Walter, you don't need to watch in the mirror. I know what I'm doing." The mustachioed barber grinned. But he obliged.

Walter donned the glasses and sat up in the chair. No doubt about it. Here stood the one he was looking for—Uncle Billy himself. This would save him a long ride. As Walter pricked up his ears, he heard Uncle Billy and the other two customers discussing the kidnapped girl and the abortive raid that had happened only last night. How had this news reached town ahead of him? It hadn't come from him or Johnny. The story must have been spread by one or both of the raiders.

"Sam, I'll be back later for the shave," Walter said, climbing laboriously from the chair and wiping the lather from his face with the drape. "Go ahead and take that next gent."

He approached Thorne. "You're the fella goes by the name of Uncle Billy?"

"That's me."

"Mind if we step outside and talk a minute?"

Walter snatched the brown felt off the hat tree as he exited. "Think I found something you lost," he said, facing Thorne in the bright sunshine.

"And what might that be?" The bewhiskered hermit peered at him from under the brim of his ratty straw.

Walter held out the hat with the hole in it.

"Don't know where you found that, but it ain't mine. Looks a mite big for me, anyway."

"Who'd you buy it for?" Walter wasn't going to play games with this old fellow.

"I didn't buy it."

"The clerk at the mercantile says you did."

"There's lots of hats look like that. I reckon he's mistook."

"I don't believe so. The clerk is an employee of mine, and he's got a very good memory for faces. Yours is a face he wouldn't forget . . . especially since he saw it yesterday."

"Mister . . . ?"

"Walter Clayton. And you know damned well who I am."

"Mister Clayton, I really don't know what you're talking about. I reckon you got me mixed up with somebody else."

"Maybe you'd like me to shoot off one of your toes . . . unless you decide to tell the truth. . . ." He put a hand to his revolver. Uncle Billy didn't appear to be armed, but one had always to look for a hideout gun.

"Grandpa!"

He turned to see Johnny running toward him with

that peculiar, limping gait. What now? he thought to himself, and then asked: "Where the hell's my newspaper, Johnny?"

"Never mind that. Silas Newburn and his sons, Tad and Martin, and two other Newburns are boarding the train.

"What's that to me? I'm not their keeper."

Johnny cast a dubious eye on Thorne, who stood nearby. He lowered his voice and guided his grandfather a few yards away. "I saw Tad loading something on the baggage car. . . ."

Uncle Billy appeared to be staring at something across the street.

". . . a case of dynamite."

"How do you know?"

"Stenciled right on the wooden crate!" Johnny was clearly exasperated.

An alarm bell rang in the back of Walter Clayton's mind. He reached for his billfold, and withdrew several greenbacks.

Thorne barely picked up the words of the deep voice. "Get aboard and find out where they're going."

"The station agent and the conductor won't tell me."

"Then use your ingenuity!" Walter snapped. "I have to know. Wire me anytime, day or night, when you find out. Now get going!"

Two blasts on the steam whistle signaled imminent departure.

Johnny snatched the bills, stuffed them into his pocket, and hurried off.

Watching him, Walter cringed at his grandson's loping run. He'd never get over the fact that Johnny

had been crippled for life by a bullet from a Newburn, just because Johnny had fallen in love with a
Newburn girl.

Johnny disappeared around the side of the depot
just as the train began chuffing and started to
move.

Walter turned around and Uncle Billy was gone.
"No matter," he muttered. "He's alerted now, but
there may be bigger things afoot."

It wasn't yet noon, but he was hungry. A mental
image of steak and potatoes made his stomach
growl. He'd ride home alone later, trailing Johnny's
mount.

As he started across the street toward a steak
house, he had an uneasy feeling in his stomach.
Why was Silas leaving town? Was this some kind of
feint to throw him off guard? He knew Silas would
never abandon his granddaughter, no matter what
she'd done to disgrace the family. Otto had sworn
he'd relayed Walter's terms perfectly—either di-
vulge the exact location of the cache, or Nellie would
die. How could the Newburns leave her in such
jeopardy? Silas knew that Walter Clayton never
bluffed. Yet, somebody—probably two of the Newburn clan—had raided his farm last night, presum-
ably in an attempt to rescue the girl. Or else they
were looking for the stolen $250,000. Should he hurt
the girl in some way to retaliate and show that he
meant what he said about an eye for an eye? Probably not. Keep the girl in good shape as the prize to
be ransomed for the pot of gold at the end of the
rainbow.

Yet, he couldn't shake the feeling that something
wasn't quite right. If Johnny had really seen what he
claimed—Tad Newburn loading a case of dynamite—

where were five members of the Newburn clan taking it?

He didn't enjoy his lunch—nagging doubt and worry causing a rare dyspepsia.

The news that awaited at his farm would make him even sicker.

Chapter Fifteen

Rapid hoof beats.

Rasmussen dropped the strip of bacon on his plate and sprang to the door of the shack, gun in hand. Thorne's mule trotted into view, and the agent reined up, leaping to the ground.

"Get your stuff together," he said, striding into the shack. "The boil is coming to a head."

"What's up?"

"Silas Newburn's heading up a grab for the cache. And Walter Clayton's on my trail because of that hat you lost." He sat down on the kitchen chair and began to pull off his brogans, relaying his encounter with the head of the Clayton clan.

Rasmussen grabbed his saddlebags and folded his spare shirt and pants into it. He had little to pack besides a toothbrush and a small box of ammunition for the Merwin-Hulbert.

"I'm betting the Newburns are headed for the New Mexico Territory, and Johnny Clayton's following them." He quoted the conversation he'd overheard between Johnny and his grandfather.

"There're liable to be some fireworks on that train before we can catch up," Rasmussen said. "When's the next westbound leave?"

"This evening. Can't risk riding back to town and running into Walter Clayton. That old man probably has the sheriff in his pocket, and he could charge me with trespassing and burglary, and delay us indefinitely while Walter waits for Johnny's telegram."

"Let's handle it this way," Rasmussen said. "We'll ride over to Lebanon, return those two rental horses, board your mule, and catch the westbound train there."

"Good thinking." Thorne went into the bedroom to finish changing clothes.

"Reckon old man Clayton can muster enough men to stop the Newburns?"

"He owns a good portion of the town, so he's got plenty of men in his employ if he chooses to use them," Thorne answered from the next room. "But I'm betting he'll want to keep something this big within his own small circle. Could be he plans to wait till Silas has the cache in hand, then try to take it from him, like Johnny and his gunmen took that two hundred and fifty thousand dollars."

Rasmussen didn't like to be reminded of that incident. "In any event, we have to get there and put a stop to this whole business." He had no idea how the two of them would accomplish such a feat. They'd have to play whatever hand they were dealt. "Almost like the North-West Mounted Police," Rasmussen commented. "The force always expected one or two men to turn back a gang of any size, whether whiskey runners, rebellious Métis, or Indians." He gave a dry chuckle. "The Mounties' motto . . . *Maintien le Droit* . . . Maintain the Right."

"By whatever means," Thorne finished, buckling the leather leggings he wore over his canvas pants.

"Better shake a leg," Rasmussen said. "We've got a train to catch, thirty miles from here."

"Wait a minute." Thorne went to the stove, poured steaming coffee from the black pot into his shaving mug. "No time to heat up more water." He lathered up and shaved his white whiskers, revealing a much younger-looking man beneath.

While Thorne grabbed a bite to eat, Rasmussen took his turn with the razor, stooping to see himself in the tiny mirror on the wall. Then he snipped his shaggy blond hair into a manageable length. He surveyed his new reflection. "That seven and three-quarter size hat would be too big for me now," he said. "Clayton would have to lay the blame on somebody else."

"We won't give him a chance to blame anybody," Thorne said, swinging the gun belt around his lean hips. "Let's go."

Rasmussen took up the reins of the led horse and swung into the saddle. He cast a last look at the unpainted shack he'd come to consider home. It wasn't as if the two of them were dashing off on some fast chase that would end in a few hours. Both he and Thorne were experienced lawmen and sensed, without discussing it, that they were in for a long, hard slog with the possibility of a fight at the end of it. A vision from five years earlier crept into his mind. He saw again a day coach on the partially finished Canadian Pacific, red-coated troops, rifles at hand, sprawled in sleep as the train rolled across the prairie toward a confrontation with the Métis rebels. Now he and Thorne were about to board a westbound train, with the odds long against them in the fight ahead.

They trotted their mounts and made good time on

the road to Lebanon in the muggy heat of early afternoon, meeting two farmers with loads of produce, heading toward Springfield.

An hour later, they were walking their horses, and spotted a horseman riding leisurely toward them. The man wore a wide-brimmed black hat.

"Watch this," Thorne said.

As the rider approached, Thorne touched the brim of his low-crowned Stetson. "Afternoon, Reverend."

The young man looked curiously at him. "Good day to you, sir," he said cordially as he passed on.

A minute later, Thorne chuckled. "That was the Reverend Harlan Ashby. I've sat in his church many a Sunday, and eaten dinner with him probably a dozen times. If he didn't recognize me, clean-shaven and dressed as somebody other than the man he knows as Uncle Billy, then it's not likely the Claytons or Newburns will know me, either."

"I was beginning to think I'd seen the last of these animals," the liveryman said, pulling the saddle off the led horse.

"Got delayed," Rasmussen said. "But they haven't had much work. Both in good shape."

"Got a mule I want to board for a week or two," Thorne said, dismounting.

A deal was struck and the two men started for the depot on the edge of town, carrying their light duffel.

"Two one-way tickets to Santa Fé," Thorne said to the agent at the window. "Pullman all the way."

"Yes, sir."

The agent prepared the tickets and the two men boarded the train that had just pulled into the station. "Not a quarter hour to spare," Thorne said.

"Why Santa Fé?"

"I'm guessing that's as far as they're likely to go. If we somehow find out they got off earlier, we can do the same. But with these tickets, we're covered."

In spite of their perilous, uncertain mission, Rasmussen relaxed in the Pullman. It was good again to experience the luxury of train travel. *"Ahhh!"* He stretched his big frame onto the reclining seat. "When this is all over, maybe I'll get a job as a conductor."

"A job? Then you'd have to work, not be waited on hand and foot as a paying customer."

Rasmussen locked his hands behind his head and grinned. "You'll have to admit these bunks sure beat that thing with the rope springs in your shack."

"You weren't complaining about my bed when I dragged you in there, half dead."

"True. I could've slept on a bed of nails at that point."

After dark, the train pulled into Springfield for a twenty-minute stop.

With Rasmussen standing close by, eyeing the men in the depot, Thorne approached the ticket agent. "You know Silas Newburn?" he inquired through the barred window.

"Yes, sir."

"He went west on the morning train. What was his party's final destination?"

"I don't know, sir. I just came on duty at four o'clock."

"You don't keep records of ticket sales?"

"Only total numbers for accounting purposes. No names. It would be an impossible paperwork job, and serve no good purpose."

"It'd serve a good purpose in this instance," Thorne muttered under his breath.

"You might be able to ask the agent who was on duty this morning . . . unless the tickets were purchased earlier than today."

"Where can I find him?"

"Bill Bunter? He's probably at home eating supper, or maybe at the Blue Bell Saloon where he goes of an evening. But you're wasting your time. Bill's close-mouthed about that sort of thing. Mister Newburn is a famous man hereabouts. I'm sure lots of folks would be curious about his comings and goings. Bill has professional pride and considers personal information just that . . . personal."

" 'Booaarrdd!' " The conductor was waving his red lantern from the caboose.

"Thanks, anyway." Thorne motioned to Rasmussen and the two men hurried to catch their departing train.

"Probably just as well he didn't have a record of the names and destinations," Thorne said as they settled into the bunks the porter had made up. "I might've been forced to show my Secret Service badge to get it. Don't want to shed my cover until I have to."

Her first cousin, Darrel Weaver, was the last person Nellie Newburn expected to see on the train. Yet, there he was—her mother's sister's son, in the flesh. She rubbed her bleary eyes and looked again at the man seated at the far end of the coach. It had to be DJ, as she'd always called him—the droopy eyes, the same long face. She'd heard that everyone in the world had a look-alike somewhere, but this was just too coincidental. She and Darrel were within a few months of the same age and even closer in attitude and outlook. Under that sad-hound face lurked a sparkling wit and personality Nellie had enjoyed all her growing-up years. Although they'd been playmates and confidants as children, she hadn't seen him in months.

Was he on some kind of business trip? A bachelor, he had a local reputation as a very intelligent man who invented games and puzzles for children and kept them fascinated with magic tricks. He was a wood carver, read voraciously, and had many avocations—but no vocation. The last time she'd seen him, he was peddling insurance in northern Arkansas for a recently founded New England company.

Her first instinct was to go speak to him. It'd been days since she'd seen a friendly face. But she hesitated. She was dirty, smelly, and broke, and he'd be sure to ask where she was going. How could she explain all this?

Just then the end door opened and the conductor came through. She dropped her eyes and pretended to study her fingernails, but sensed his stopping next to her seat.

"We'll be in Sapulpa in thirty minutes," he said quietly. "And I'll have to collect your ticket for points west. Or, you'll have to get off." He was silent for a moment, then leaned down close. He voice was a whisper. "Or, you might have something personal to trade for a ticket, as we discussed earlier."

She looked up. He had the trace of a smile on his lips as he moved down the aisle. As soon as he'd passed out of the car, she decided to get up and go to her cousin. He was reading a book and didn't see her approach. She took a deep breath and assumed a cheerful attitude. "Why, DJ, I didn't expect to see you here!"

His face lit up with a huge grin. "Nellie! Plop your ass down here, gal. You're a welcome sight for these old eyes."

"Your eyes are no older than mine," she reminded him as she slid into the vacant side of the double seat.

He reached around and gave her a hug. "Running from something?" he asked.

"Is it that obvious?"

"Nellie, you're talking to your cousin DJ. I've known you since we were both knee-high to a praying mantis."

She giggled in spite of herself. "You could always make me laugh." She was feeling better already, and wondered why she'd even hesitated rushing to greet him.

"Before I ask what you're doing here, I think you need a drink." He surreptitiously produced a silver flask from an inside coat pocket.

She glanced around to see if anyone was watching before she uncapped it and took a swig. The brandy burned a path to her empty stomach. Her childhood desire to share in some innocent mischief suddenly returned. Despite the disapproving frown of an elderly woman across the aisle, she took another swallow. "*Whew!* That's good. But it'll go right to my head."

"Good. It'll loosen you up. Now," he said, taking a nip himself, then capping the flask, "you go first and don't leave out any details."

Nellie filled him in on her life, beginning with her selection to be courier for the $250,000 from the Canadian bank. It was good to have a friend to confide in; she hardly paused for breath while her story spilled out in a continuous stream. She brought him up to date with her boarding the train the day before, and the conductor's proposition.

"I'll have to say my story can't top that," Darrel said when she finally came to a stop. "I've been working, selling out of town a lot, trying to stay out of the way of flying bullets and any part of family troubles."

"But you are part of it," she reminded him. She lowered her voice so that only he could hear. "You and Grandpa Silas are the only ones alive who still know the exact location of that cold cache."

"To my everlasting regret. I'm still carrying a piece of lead in my back from that expedition out West. Wish I'd never let the old man bribe me into going. But . . . I was broke at the time." He shrugged. "A man will do 'most anything for money if you catch him at a low point."

"Why are you here now?" she asked.

"Same reason. I'm selling on commission, and nobody wants to buy insurance. Truth be told, I'm the world's worst salesman." He smiled ruefully, and she suddenly felt sorry for him.

"You mean you're on this train because Grandpa Silas sent you after that treasure again?"

Darrel nodded. "Only this time, he came along, too, in addition to your uncles, Tad and Martin, and another man from his castle."

"What? They're on this train?" Her stomach contracted.

"Two cars ahead in the Pullman."

"I have to hide. They mustn't see me. I tried to run away. I've got to get off." She slid down in the seat.

"How much money do you have?" he asked.

She dropped her eyes. "A dollar. Spent two dollars yesterday on food from a vendor at a depot stop."

He pressed several gold coins into her hand. She caught her breath when she saw four double eagles. "I can't take this."

"You can and you will. Part of my advance. I haven't earned it yet. You think I'd leave you in such a fix?"

She could feel tears welling up in her eyes.

"Look, you said you wanted to start a new life . . . possibly get a job as a Harvey Girl."

She nodded, not trusting herself to speak.

"Then get off at the next stop. I'll take care of that conductor. Clean up, buy some clothes, and a decent meal. Catch the next train if you want to. That will get you away from Silas and the others."

"OK."

"We're going on to Santa Fé," he said, taking her hand. "Silas plans to buy two wagons and mule teams, then we'll head into the northern part of the territory. I don't care anything about that treasure, but I'm under oath not to reveal the exact location, and I'll respect that pledge."

She shuddered. "I don't want to know, anyway."

"It might be a while before we see each other," he said with feeling. "God, I'm glad to see you." He looked her up and down. Then he sighed, and turned away. "I believed we could get away with the treasure this time. But . . . now I'm not so sure. You were supposed to be held for ransom in exchange for the treasure map. Now that you're loose, and Walter Clayton has probably figured out we made a run around them, he and his clan will be hot on our trail."

"You think there'll be another fight if they catch up?"

"I don't know. But I'm not risking my life again to preserve a lot of cold metal . . . gold and silver that will be used to split this country. You know what it's like to get most of the family down on you."

"Yes."

"I won't fight. If it comes to that, I'll make a run for it. Disappear somewhere . . . if I survive once the shooting starts."

They looked fondly at each other. "Oh, DJ, what's happened to us? How did we come to this?"

An impish grin appeared on his face as if he had a secret solution he was about to share with her. "It'll be all right, Nellie. Don't you worry. We'll look back on this someday, and laugh. Something exciting to entertain our kids and grandkids."

"If we ever have any," she replied tearfully.

"Come on. We'll be in Sapulpa shortly. I want you off this train before anyone spots you." He took her arm and ushered her toward the back of the car.

"DJ, where will you be? I want to repay this money."

"Consider it a deposit on the future."

"But you wouldn't have come on this expedition if you hadn't needed the money yourself."

"The old man is good for it. He's covering all our expenses. Mine were just a little heavier than expected."

He opened the door and stepped out ahead of her. Steel couplings were *clattering,* the wheels *clicking* and jarring over the uneven roadbed. A warm wind whipped around between the cars. She could feel the train slowing, but they were still rolling about twenty miles an hour.

The end door of the next car opened, and a small, dark man stepped out onto the platform. He looked up and his mouth dropped open. "Nellie!"

Darrel reacted swiftly at the sight of Johnny Clayton. He sprang across the four feet between them, grabbed Johnny by the collar, and yanked. When the smaller man stumbled forward, off balance, Darrel spun him around, snatched him by the back of his belt, and heaved. Johnny went flying off the train.

"Oh, God!" Nellie gasped, watching him sliding and tumbling down the grassy embankment.

"Can't stop and think about it," Darrel said, his droopy eyes wide. "After what that guy has done to you, he can afford to walk a ways."

"What was he doing here?" she cried, her head in a whirl. "I didn't know he was on this train."

"Guess he's been lying low, maybe following our party. Good riddance, in any case. The train stops only a few minutes in Sapulpa. He won't have time to catch up."

The door burst open behind them. "What's going on here?" the conductor demanded, grabbing Darrel by the shoulder. "You threw that man off the train! I'll have you arrested!" he shouted above the rushing wind.

Darrel pulled loose from the man's grasp and stepped back. "Is he the one?" he asked Nellie.

"Yes."

"Oops! Sorry." Darrel bowled his shoulder into the uniformed man, who fell backward from the unexpected blow, grabbing the iron railing with one hand to keep from falling. Darrel's leg whipped up, kicking the conductor's grip off the railing.

"Aagghh!" The conductor's cap flew off and his arms wind-milled in a futile effort to save his balance as he cart-wheeled backward, bouncing and sliding in the gravel ballast away from the train.

"Oh, my God, DJ, you've killed both of them."

"Not likely. Maybe bruised them up a bit, if they didn't break anything." He leaned out and looked back along the right of way. Pulling in his head, he said: "Never saw two clumsier men. They have to be more careful on these swaying platforms."

The look of innocent wonder on his long face was too much for her; she burst out laughing.

Chapter Sixteen

When Kent Rasmussen awoke in his upper berth, he wasn't sure where he was. Not even his healing back wound had kept him from deep sleep. He pulled aside the curtain and looked out at a flat, treeless terrain sliding past. For a moment, until fully awake, he saw the flat plain of the Texas panhandle as the prairies of western Canada.

He yawned and stretched, then leaned over the edge of the bunk. "Alex . . . ?" He stopped. Thorne was up and gone. Rasmussen fished in his pants, folded near his head, and pulled out his watch. It had stopped. "Too busy to wind it," he muttered, shoving it away.

Then: "Kent, get up."

"What?" The urgency of Thorne's voice startled him, and he pushed up on his elbow. "What's wrong?"

"Have to show you something."

"Can it wait till I dress?"

"Yeah. Hurry."

Icy fingers clutched at his stomach. In the confined space of the upper berth, Rasmussen pulled on his shirt and struggled into his pants. What could've happened, now? He stepped down, buckled his belt, and reached to pull on his boots.

Thorne stood by with a strange look on his face. "Come with me." He led the way into the adjacent dining car. "We're having an early breakfast." He stepped aside. There sat Nellie Newburn.

For a moment, Rasmussen couldn't speak. Nellie sprang up and suddenly they were embracing, his face buried in her fragrant hair.

Finally she pulled back, face radiant. She looked great. He couldn't take his eyes from her as they all sat down to breakfast.

Thorne had already ordered, and the white-coated waiter showed up with scrambled eggs, bacon, and toast.

"What a way to start the day!" was all Rasmussen could think to say. He took a sip of coffee. Food was secondary as he stared at her. "You're a vision."

"I thought you were dead," she said between bites.

"They did their best."

"I was on the porch and heard the shot, but didn't know. . . ." She stopped, seeming to choke up at the memory. "Were you hurt badly?"

"No. It's about healed." Only a slight exaggeration. He nodded at Thorne. "This man saved my life."

"I couldn't believe my eyes when I saw her here this morning," Thorne said. "I couldn't keep her in suspense. Had to tell her you were with me."

"He doesn't look much like Uncle Billy," she said to Rasmussen. Then to Thorne: "You sure had me fooled."

"And everybody else," Rasmussen said. "But we were taken in by a professional."

"I just knew you were dead when I overheard

Grandpa Silas say he was glad the Claytons had put you out of the picture. That ended my respect for my grandfather, and I decided I had to take your advice and get away from there. A few miles from town, Johnny and Black Rogers kidnapped me." She paled slightly at the recollection. "You two could have been killed in that rescue attempt. They had me locked down in the fruit cellar." She went on to detail her escape. "I managed to get on the train that's ten or twelve hours ahead of us, and stayed out of sight for a day before I ran into my cousin, Darrel Weaver."

"He's the one you told me knew the location of the treasure?" Rasmussen interjected.

"That's the one. In fact, he's with Grandpa Silas, Uncle Tad, Uncle Martin, and another knight, and they're going after the treasure. If it weren't for DJ . . . that's what I call Darrel . . . I wouldn't be here now. He gave me money, and I got off in a little town, cleaned up, ate, bought some new clothes, and caught the next train . . . this one. I slept sitting up last night," she added.

"Amazing," Rasmussen breathed, his respect for this woman growing.

"To complicate things further," she said, "Johnny Clayton was on that train. I don't know how or why. . . ."

"I do," Thorne said. "I was talking to Walter Clayton when the old man ordered Johnny to follow and report where the Newburns were going."

"DJ told me they were heading for Santa Fé," she said. "Then overland by wagon to the northern part of the territory. He wouldn't say exactly where."

"As soon as Johnny finds this out, he'll telegraph Walter, and the chase will be on for sure," Thorne said.

She nodded thoughtfully. "If Johnny's not hurt too badly. . . ."

"What do you mean?"

She told them about her cousin throwing both Johnny and the offensive conductor off the train.

"Damn! I've got to meet this cousin of yours. He must be one helluva man," Rasmussen said.

"My best friend, growing up." She sighed. "I'd die if anything happened to him. He was the only Newburn survivor of the last raid on that cold cache a few years ago, and he agreed to come along this time only because he was broke."

The train slowed. Rasmussen glanced absently out the window, his mind churning with other thoughts. "After all that's happened . . . my getting shot, your kidnapping, our failed rescue attempt, then Walter Clayton tracking my hat to Thorne, I figure it must be time for a little good luck. Didn't know it was going to be this good."

The luck wasn't destined to last.

Ten minutes later, Rasmussen stood beside the train, hair whipping in the dry Texas wind. "What's the hold-up?"

The portly conductor shielded his eyes from the grit, and secured his pillbox cap with the other hand. "Flash flood weakened the support beams o' that log trestle. Can't get over the arroyo till it's shored up."

"How long?"

"Depends on how quick a repair crew gets here on a handcar. We're just now sending a wire ahead to the next town for help."

Rasmussen saw one of the trainmen climbing a nearby pole to clip on a wire from their portable telegraph key.

"Four hours, I'd say," the conductor continued.

"Should put us in Santa Fé about . . ."—he consulted his nickel-plated watch—"nine in the morning, if we don't run into more trouble."

"Thanks." Rasmussen climbed back into the Pullman to inform Thorne and Nellie.

"Shouldn't matter," Thorne said. "As it is, we're only a few hours behind. It'll take 'em a day or so to get provisioned and secure wagons and mules. We don't want to come in on top of them."

As it turned out, the repairs took nine hours, so the train didn't pull into the Santa Fé depot until 3:10 the next afternoon.

Rasmussen was feeling dragged out. He'd given his bunk to Nellie and slept as best he could on a double seat in the day coach. Now his wound was hurting again. But as they stepped down from the train, grips in hand, he didn't care. It was a warm, sleepy afternoon and the old town appeared as if it had not seen an exciting day since the Pueblo revolt 200 years earlier. They wandered into the plaza that had once been the terminus of the Santa Fé Trail.

"They've been here and gone," Rasmussen said. "Any idea where?" He looked at Nellie.

"Wish I'd pressed DJ into telling me more," she said. "But my only idea then was to get away. Didn't realize I'd be following them."

"Let's start at the livery stables and see if they rented some mules and wagons."

She shook her head. "He'd buy them. Grandpa has money and wouldn't stint on buying whatever he needed. If they were going to load up the wagons with treasure, they wouldn't be bringing them back."

"Even if they were going to off-load the stuff onto a train and transport it back to Missouri?" Rasmussen asked. "I can't imagine hauling anything that heavy overland by wagon. If this cache is as big as reported, they surely wouldn't try to haul it very far by wagon. I assume most of it is in the form of bullion or coin. Unless it's sealed tight in something weatherproof, paper money wouldn't hold up."

"Did your grandfather say how he planned to transport it? Or where he planned to take it?" Thorne asked.

It was the first time Rasmussen had considered the post-discovery problem.

The three of them looked blankly at each other.

"All DJ said was they were going to the northern part of the territory."

"Fairly mountainous north of here," Thorne said. "Might be they're going to take a string of pack mules."

Nellie frowned. "DJ said they were going with wagons. In fact, he said Silas was going to buy them."

"If they suspected your cousin wasn't loyal, Silas and Tad might not have told him everything."

"No. Grandpa Silas isn't devious like that."

"Except when dealing with you," Rasmussen said.

She shrugged. "That's because, long ago, I proved I couldn't be trusted when I ran off with Johnny Clayton."

They stood on the grassy plaza and gazed at the quiet, dusty streets. There was no sign of unusual activity anywhere. Pedestrians were coming and going. Indians lounged in the shade of an arched portico, offering a variety of handmade items to tourists who'd descended from the train. A block away, a large cathedral dominated the view at the end of a street.

"They arrived here a day and a half ago," Rasmussen said. "Unless they picked up more men . . . teamsters and the like . . . there were only five in their party. Wouldn't have taken them long to get going, especially if they had telegraphed ahead to buy wagons, mules, and provisions. Let's get to checking."

A search of the town's livery stables proved futile. No one had bought or rented any wagons or mule teams in the past two days. By the time they'd canvassed all the places they could think of, it was past 5:00. Even clerks in the mercantile and grocery stores denied seeing any such party.

"You reckon they got delayed somewhere and haven't arrived, or maybe got off the train somewhere else?" Rasmussen speculated as they came out of the last livery. "Nobody seems to have seen them."

"Grandpa Silas has friends in this part of the country," Nellie said. "Rich friends who could have supplied him with wagons and teams. I've heard him refer to at least two who own ranches in the area. They're not town people."

"That's probably it," Thorne said, brightening up. "Silas had no need of livery stables like common folk."

"But wouldn't that mean that he'd have to let more people in on this mission?" Rasmussen asked. "Wouldn't his wealthy friends be curious?"

"No need to speculate about all that," Thorne said. "Let's get horses and head north while the trail is warm. Be more comfortable if we rented a buggy. But there's rough terrain north of here where a buggy couldn't travel," he added, glancing at Nellie.

"And wagons could?"

"We don't know their plans, so we should be prepared for anything," Thorne said. "There's a good road northwest to Taos but, as I recollect, that's more than sixty miles away. Let's find a hotel and a meal and rest up. Start fresh in the morning. As long as we don't know exactly where they're heading, it's best we have plenty of daylight.

At sunup next morning they rented three saddle horses and started north along a well-traveled sandy road. It proved to be a long, tiring day in the saddle with no sign of their quarry, even though there were good views of the terrain in nearly every direction. They paced themselves, pausing four times to rest and stretch their legs and let the horses graze on the sparse vegetation.

In late afternoon, they reached the ancient pueblo of Taos where they stopped for nearly an hour to rest, lounging by a public well while the horses drank their fill from a stone trough.

Rasmussen propped a foot on a nearby stone parapet, sniffing a breeze that carried the faint scent of desert vegetation. "Notice how sharp and clear everything looks," he remarked. "No haze or dust in the air."

"No moisture in the air to filter the sunlight," Thorne replied. "At this elevation, without the protective blanket of humidity, you'll also feel the temperature drop sharply at night."

Rasmussen nodded, gazing at the dun-colored buildings that blended with the surrounding desert.

As they rode out, they could smell tantalizing aromas of roasting meat wafting from across adobe walls and hidden patios, but no one mentioned stopping to eat. There was a sense of urgency to cover as much ground as possible in hope of picking up the trail of the Newburn party. They were operating only on Darrel's vague statement that the treasure lay north of Santa Fé.

By the time they reached the village of Río Colorado, twenty miles north of Taos, the sun had declined behind the San Juan Mountains. The trio reined up in front of a small grocery.

"We've been taking it pretty easy, but these horses are about done in," Rasmussen said, dismounting stiffly.

"They're not the only ones," Nellie remarked.

"We'll buy something to eat, and make a few inquiries," Thorne said, leading the way.

"May I be of help to you?" a middle-aged Mexican greeted them from atop a stool where he was lighting a hanging Rochester lamp. He turned up the wick and soft light radiated downward into the room, reflected by a wide, brass shade.

Rasmussen noted the man's impassive face, scarred by old pockmarks. In the lamplight he saw a tiny cross tattooed on the Mexican's forehead, just below the receding black hair.

"Ten sticks of jerky and a loaf of bread," Thorne said, surveying the canned goods and sacks of beans and flour lining the walls. The room had a pleasant blend of aromas—spices, coffee, wood smoke.

Thorne dug into his pocket for money while Rasmussen leaned his elbows on the counter. "Is there a hotel or boarding house nearby?" he asked.

The dark-skinned man ripped a length of brown wrapping paper from a roll and began folding it around the bread and meat. "Sí. Up the street. I think you will find it to your liking."

The storekeeper took Thorne's money, made

change from a cash drawer, and handed back some coins, all the while keeping his eyes downcast as if to avoid looking directly at them. When he did glance up, his eyes seemed to smolder with some inner fire—a blaze the man took pains to bank.

"Anything else I can do for you?" he asked politely, ignoring Nellie who stood by the door.

"We're trying to catch up with five men who might have come this way a day or so ago," Thorne said casually.

"Were these men Anglos or Mexicans?"

"Anglos."

"*¿Amigos?*" the storekeeper inquired quietly, his arresting eyes staring at the floor.

Thorne and Rasmussen looked at each other. Should they tell him the truth in hopes of getting a truthful answer? They seemed to read each other's expressions.

"They're no friends of ours," Thorne said.

"They're going after stolen money . . . a large amount of gold and silver," Rasmussen added while Thorne pulled out his small leather folder with his card, badge, and photograph, identifying him as a Secret Service agent.

"The leader of these men is the grandfather of this young lady," Thorne said, indicating Nellie.

The storekeeper shot a penetrating glance at Nellie, then looked back at Thorne's identification. "Ah . . . then all is not well in her family."

"That's right. These men are enemies of the United States government, and we must stop them."

"Who does the money belong to?" the storekeeper inquired, with more interest than before.

Rasmussen felt they had set the hook. This man knew something.

"It's stolen Army payrolls . . . a good deal of it was taken from the treasury of the former Confederate States of America, and a lot more came from bandits who've robbed banks and trains over the last thirty years," Thorne told him.

"If we don't stop them," Rasmussen said, "they'll use the money to bribe the Mexican government into becoming part of a new country made up of a few Southern states and Caribbean islands. They call that whole area The Golden Circle."

Before the Mexican could respond, Thorne added: "If you've seen these men, you'd be doing a great service to your country by telling us where they are."

Even though this was the New Mexico Territory, a possession of the United States, it had been part of Mexico just over a generation ago, and Rasmussen couldn't guess where this man's loyalties lay.

The Mexican storekeeper turned and called over his shoulder: "Blanco!"

A slender dark boy, who looked to be on the underside of twelve, trotted out of a back room. The proprietor spoke to him in rapid Spanish. The boy nodded and hurried out the front door.

"I have taken the liberty of sending the boy to notify *Señora* O'Reilly you will be staying at her hotel tonight," he said.

"Gracias."

The Mexican came around the counter, locked his front door, and pulled down the shade. "It is my custom to close at sundown for one hour to eat supper, because my store remains open during the usual *siesta* period in early afternoon," he explained.

It was not as uncomfortably stuffy in the closed store as Rasmussen had expected. A high window in the wall let in the evening breeze.

"Sit, *por favor.*" The storekeeper motioned to several wooden chairs.

The room reminded Rasmussen of an Ozark country store, with its captain's chairs and potbellied stove.

"My name is Luis Ortiz," the man began. "I own this store. For a time I was mayor of Río Colorado, where I live now for many years." He folded his arms and leaned against the counter. "I know where are these *hombres* you seek. They camp ten miles west, near Tres Lobos Cañon. I show you tonight . . . or *mañana,* if you wish."

"How did you know they were nearby?" Rasmussen asked, sensing deception.

"Shepherds in Tres Lobos Cañon say they see strange men with wagons in the dark of night." He smiled. "Word of their presence has spread through the village. Superstitious old women came into my store today to tell me these men were ghostly members of the brotherhood, returning to their *morada.* I pointed out that ghosts do not travel by wagon."

"Why would they even think these were ghosts?" Rasmussen asked.

"Sometimes, over twenty years, *más o menos,* men, ghosts . . . or figures of some kind . . . nobody knows . . . were seen at night around the entrance to Tres Lobos Cañon. These reports came from all kinds of people . . . mostly sober men who do not lie. I never saw the figures myself, but many witnesses, during many years, telling the same story cannot be passed off as drunken visions, or wild animals, or shadows. These pious old women have just decided among themselves that the visions were ghosts of dead brothers."

Rasmussen was confused, but Thorne said: "Now

I understand that tiny cross on your forehead. You're a member of the *Penitentes*."

"*Sí*. For years I was the *hermano* mayor here. Now I'm only a humble brother."

"You'll have to explain that," Rasmussen said.

"The Brothers of Our Father, Jesus, is an order of Catholic laymen of Spanish descent," Thorne said with a glance toward Ortiz. "I know of them from my time in Arizona and New Mexico ten years ago."

"That is correct, *Señor* . . . ?

"Thorne. Alex Thorne."

"*Señor* Thorne is right. We have a tradition from Spain and Mexico. The order grew strong when the Spanish empire became weak and the Franciscan friars left the frontier more than a hundred years ago. When our people had no priests, *Los Hermanos* became a way for them to hold onto the faith. Many centuries ago, while Saint Francis lived, he started the Third Order for lay people. The men of our *morada* practice charity, help those in need, avoid saloons, and the carrying of weapons. We try to live our Christian faith," Ortiz said with a hint of pride.

"What was that name you called them a minute ago?" Rasmussen asked.

"*Penitentes*," Ortiz said. "That is what outsiders call us because we do bodily penance, usually during Holy Week."

"Self-flagellation," Thorne explained. "Outsiders think whipping one's bare back is a bloody, barbaric practice, but it's a tradition of self-mortification that goes back at least to the Thirteen Hundreds when the Black Death killed half of Europe."

"Even the bishop does not agree with this old, revered practice," Ortiz said. "He says our penance injures our God-given bodies. But *Los Hermanos* believe our rites should not be banned. We chant the litanies in our processions, and select one among us, who is worthy, to take the part of the Cristo, in our passion play. He is tied to a cross for a time. Imitating the sufferings of Christ is a holy thing to do." Ortiz made a quick sign of the cross.

"Their secrecy generates suspicion and condemnation from outsiders . . . even the Catholic hierarchy," Thorne said. "Those flagellants who march in the Good Friday Stations of the Cross are hooded, and outsiders think it's sinister."

"Our brothers do not hide from the Church," Ortiz explained. "They wish only to be humble in their penance and not show off for others."

"All very interesting, but what's this got to do with the Newburn party?" Rasmussen cut in.

"Would I help three Anglo strangers for no reason?" Ortiz flashed a look at Rasmussen with smoldering eyes. "Politicians and outsiders who would destroy *Los Hermanos* say we are affiliated with *Las Gorras Blancas*, The White Caps, a gang of white-hooded Mexican night riders who burn and destroy, and scatter livestock. They say they discourage whites from moving onto Mexican landholdings. But they burn and loot their own people as well.

"Shepherds from Tres Lobos Cañon tell of five men they saw. This has stirred fears in our village that the five are White Hats, come to raid. And because they camp near the *morada*, many long-tongued gossips accuse the brothers of joining them. . . ."

"Morada?" Rasmussen interrupted.

"A *Penitente* meeting house, or church," Thorne explained.

"Our *morada* is near by Tres Lobos Cañon, a few miles west. I will take you there."

When Ortiz stopped speaking, Thorne said: "Since you've been open with us, I'll tell you the story of these five men." He went on to detail the feuding families, the various sources of the treasure, and what Silas Newburn and the Knights of the Golden Circle planned to do with this vast fortune—the ripping apart of several political entities to form yet another one.

"This fighting over land will never stop," Ortiz said with a slow shake of his head. "I would have New Mexico remain a part of old Mexico where my Spanish ancestors came from. But history is filled with one people dominating another, century after century. It is the way of man. I do not object to the United States taking New Mexico by force. I must live and do the best I can. Even Christ came to the Jews when they were ruled by the brutal Romans. Perhaps these things happen to keep us humble. *¿Quién sabe?*" Ortiz straightened up from lounging against the counter and went to peer out the window. "Darkness is coming. Take your belongings to the hotel. I keep my store open for two more hours. Come to my back door at ten o'clock. Then we will go."

"Gracias," Rasmussen said.

"Do not thank me. I do this for *Los Hermanos* as well as for you."

Rasmussen opened the door for Nellie and Thorne. Deepening shadows filled the dusty streets. Overhead, the sun's last rays gilded the edge of clouds sliding in from the northwest.

They led their mounts along the street without speaking, entertaining individual thoughts. Rasmussen wondered how he'd confront the man who'd ambushed him—Black Rogers. Would Darrel Weaver, Nellie's reluctant cousin, be caught in the crossfire if a battle ensued? Silas had brought his two sons, Tad and Martin. Who was the fifth knight? Someone young and reckless—perhaps a good gunman? And where was Johnny Clayton? If he'd survived his fall from the moving train, he had no doubt telegraphed Walter Clayton by now that the Newburn party's destination was Santa Fé. If Johnny had reached Santa Fé, was he also confounded about Silas's whereabouts? Maybe Johnny would hunker down and lick his wounds and wait for his grandfather to bring reinforcements.

As darkness settled over the village of Río Colorado, Rasmussen had many questions. Surely the night would bring some answers.

Chapter Seventeen

Luis Ortiz closed the back door of his store.

"You forgot to lock it," Thorne reminded him.

"Not necessary," Ortiz said. "No one in this village steals from me. We don't lock our houses." He shrugged, adding: "If they take something from my store without paying, they need it more than I do, and are welcome to it. I just don't want the White Caps to burn my store."

Unlike many buildings in the village, his store was built of wood, rather than adobe.

"Are there any around here?" Rasmussen asked.

"Yes. The White Caps have made many raids. Most of the men who hide behind white hoods are lazy Mexicans. They don't work, even in summer when there are many jobs," he said with disgust.

"There will always be people like that," Rasmussen said.

"Where are your horses?" Ortiz asked. "Too far to walk."

"In the hotel stable. They're in no shape for any more work tonight. They carried us many miles today."

"Then come. We take my buckboard."

They followed the storekeeper to his house a block

away and waited outside while he went in and spoke to his wife. Through the partially open door, Rasmussen saw a mature woman with gray hair, speaking rapid Spanish, and gesturing. Her manner indicated she wasn't happy.

Ortiz came out and closed the door. "Help me hitch the mules." He pointed to a barn in the dim light.

Fifteen minutes later, the unsprung buckboard bounced across the road and away from the scattered buildings of the village. Ortiz drove, Thorne on the seat beside him, with Rasmussen and Nellie sitting on the flat boards of the wagon, hanging on as best they could.

The night was dark, with no hint of moon or stars to light their way. Rasmussen looked up. The sky was obscured by a thick overcast—a cloud cover had slid in on a high altitude wind at dusk. *Just as well*, he thought. Apparently Ortiz knew the way so well he kept the mules at a trot. It was almost as if he were driving in daylight.

"Hang on. River ahead," Ortiz said as the buckboard rattled and bounced down a long, rocky slope.

Gripping the back of the seat, Rasmussen twisted to look forward. Were they on some sort of road, or just going cross-country? The wagon pitched down a steep bank and splashed into water. Before Rasmussen could catch his breath from the cold spray, the mules were lunging up the opposite bank. That was a river? He'd forgotten that Western rivers were usually the size of creeks in wetter climes.

They rolled on for what seemed like four or five miles. Finally Ortiz pulled up, looped the reins around the rim of the front wheel, and climbed down. "This is close enough. We go on foot from here."

Ortiz led them through the brushy landscape,

twisting and turning until they'd gone another mile. He paused and turned to them in the dark. "We must be silent from here. Our *morada* is up ahead. Make no noise. Follow me," he whispered. "Watch and listen."

In the blackness, Rasmussen sensed something blacker bulking up ahead of them. They crept ahead and felt the cold stone wall of the *morada*. Easing along to the corner, they saw a pinpoint of light in the distance. Firelight. A campfire. Rasmussen's heart began to beat faster. Their quarry was finally in sight. Or, at least he hoped it was the five men they sought.

"They've likely got a guard posted," Thorne whispered.

Rasmussen put a hand to his gun butt. These men would not hesitate to kill anyone who tried to interfere with their finding the treasure. He wondered if Ortiz was armed. Not likely, if he truly followed the practices of *Los Hermanos*. He and Thorne and Nellie each had a loaded revolver in case they were discovered. Rasmussen wished for at least a small amount of light so they could get an idea of who and what surrounded that campfire. They needed to get closer.

Fortunately Ortiz was familiar with the terrain. After a whispered consultation, they decided that Nellie would stay at the *morada* and stand watch while Ortiz led the two lawmen toward the camp.

Watching Ortiz creep ahead, Rasmussen wondered if the man's Mexican ancestors shared Indian blood. The middle-aged storekeeper seemed to slither along with cat-like grace reminiscent of Indians in the western Canadian provinces.

Rasmussen was concerned with being seen by some lone sentry. If the men at the camp hadn't posted a look-out, they were either tired or felt secure from any interference by the locals. And it was unlikely they knew of any imminent pursuit from Missouri.

Screened by desert shrubbery, the trio stole to within yards of the campfire. In the flickering firelight, three blanket-covered forms lay on the ground. One man sat on a rock, feeding small sticks to the blaze. He got up and poured himself a cup of coffee from a blackened pot setting on an iron spider over the fire. He sat back down, blowing on the steaming cup, blanket draped over his shoulders against the night chill. A carbine leaned against the rock where he sat. Firelight shone up under the man's hat. The long face and the hooded, sleepy eyes were not familiar. Rasmussen drew a deep breath. One of the Golden Circle knights, he supposed. A very lackadaisical way of keeping watch—sitting, half asleep in the full light of the fire.

Thorne nudged him and pointed at the forms on the ground, then at the sentry, and held up four fingers. He shrugged as if wondering where the fifth man might be.

Rasmussen felt a chill that wasn't due to the night air. The fifth man was out there somewhere. Just then, another figure moved out of the darkness from behind a parked wagon.

"Silas Newburn," Thorne muttered softly as the lean man tossed a sack onto the ground and said something to the guard.

There was no doubt they'd found the men they sought. It would be easy to arrest the five right now. Rasmussen whispered his idea to Thorne.

Thorne shook his head and pointed at one of the big Army supply wagons backed up to the firelight, tailgate down. The heavy, gray wagon was empty.

They didn't yet have the treasure and were technically innocent until caught with the stolen money.

The best chance he and Thorne would ever have to capture this group was now. Even if they could somehow legally detain the Newburns on suspicion, the location of the treasure would remain secret. He and Thorne and Nellie would have to wait and give the Newburns room and time to acquire the stolen property.

He nodded to Thorne and Ortiz, and began creeping soundlessly away.

They paused again near the *morada* when the fire was again a pinpoint of light in the distance.

"Did you see them?" Nellie asked in a low voice.

"Yes." Rasmussen described the look-out in detail.

"That was my cousin, DJ," she said a little sadly. "I was hoping he'd decided not to go through with this."

"Reckon he gets paid only if he does his job," Thorne said.

They retreated to the buckboard. Ortiz drove them back to the village. Even though the Mexican didn't ask for anything, Thorne slipped several folded greenbacks into his hand as they parted.

The three were silent as they walked back to the hotel. Rasmussen, for one, was exhausted. They'd been up for more than twenty hours, and covered many miles.

Thorne went into their room.

"Rap on the wall if you need anything," Rasmussen told Nellie, giving her a quick hug at the door of her adjacent room. A single lamp in a wall sconce burned low, casting a dim light in the hallway of the adobe hotel.

"Oh, Kent, what are we going to do?" she asked, her voice quavering.

"You've been tough and held up this far," he said. "Don't let it get you down. We're all tired. Things will look better in the morning. Get a good sleep." He leaned forward and kissed her lightly.

The next day, at the store, Rasmussen asked Ortiz: "Have any of those men come into town since they've been here?"

Before answering, the storekeeper watched a customer depart with a twist of chewing tobacco.

"No. Santiago, a shepherd, is a cousin of mine. He will keep watch on them for me."

"Can he do it without them knowing they're being watched?"

"*Sí.* He is a good man. I told him . . . report to me every day. His dog will guard the flock when he rides to town."

"How long do we wait?" Nellie asked. "What are they doing out there?"

"I wish I knew," Thorne said. "But we can't risk spying on them in daylight. Who owns the land beyond the *morada*?"

"Railroad property right of way."

"Railroad?" Rasmussen was all ears.

"The Denver and Río Grande runs north to Alamosa from Santa Fé."

"That explains how they got here so quickly with wagons and teams," Thorne said.

"The quarry and Tres Lobos Cañon and all land west, including the mountain range, is under control of the territorial government," Ortiz said.

"What quarry? I didn't see a quarry."

"It was dark. The abandoned quarry is a mile or more beyond their camp, inside the mouth of Tres

Lobos. In Eighteen Forty, before I came, the stone to build our *morada* was cut there. Nobody has used the quarry for many years. The workers struck water and had to abandon it." He smiled. "The children say it is bottomless. The rain and snow keep it filled with more than eighty feet of water. It's dangerous. Every summer, one or two drown while swimming there. Usually they're drunk."

"Are there any caves in that area?" Thorne asked.

Ortiz looked thoughtful. "A few, but small ones only, in the rock walls of the cañon."

"Nothing near ground level, big enough to hold a wagon?" Thorne persisted.

"No."

"To hide a large treasure they'd need a large, well-hidden hole," Rasmussen said. "And, I'm thinking, it would also have to be accessible to a man on horseback."

"Which means it couldn't be high up on some cliff wall."

"Not likely."

Rasmussen instinctively trusted Ortiz, or he would not have been openly discussing possible treasure locations. The fact is they needed his help and his knowledge.

The men were silent for a minute, then Rasmussen said: "I'm betting it won't be longer than another day . . . two at the most . . . before Walter Clayton brings his men here. We need to make a move before they show up." He paced to the front display window and looked out at the street.

"Can't do a thing until they have that treasure in hand," Thorne said.

Rasmussen nodded, his mind distracted with thoughts of forces that were about to collide in the mountains of northern New Mexico. He could sense it coming. There had to be some way to prevent an all-out battle. But how? He turned back to the others. "Look, those men out there think I'm dead. Nellie's cousin, Darrel, has never seen me. Neither have Silas's two sons, or the other Golden Circle knight. So Silas Newburn is the only one who knows what I look like. When that shepherd, Santiago, comes into the village today, I'm going back there with him, disguised as a sheepherder." He looked at Ortiz. "Your cousin may be good and reliable, but we need a trained lawman to keep an eye on the Newburns. Besides, Santiago has a flock to tend. I don't, but I could pretend to."

"I have more practice at changing identities," Thorne said. "I'll go."

"He's right," Ortiz put in. "You're too big and too blond to pass for a Mexican shepherd."

"Why do either of you have to go?" Nellie asked.

"Because they could snatch the treasure and slip away without us ever knowing in time. Remember how we thought we'd have no trouble picking up their trail at Santa Fé . . . but we couldn't? We were just lucky to find them here."

Rasmussen noticed Ortiz frowning at Nellie. Then he realized the Mexican wasn't used to women in his culture voicing opinions when men were discussing business. Perhaps the wife railing at him the night before was an exception. Rasmussen had to turn away to keep his smile from showing.

Ortiz turned to Thorne. "If you must accompany Santiago, I can transform you into a Mexican shepherd. You have gray hair and a smaller body. It will take only a poncho and a staff and an old hat."

"Good."

"*Señor* Rasmussen, I have a bushel of walnuts in the back room. I can use the hulls to stain your face and hands dark enough to be one of our heritage, so you can pass for one of *Los Hermanos*. You and I can go to the *morada* and keep watch from there."

Thorne raised his eyebrows. "Aren't outsiders strictly forbidden to enter a *morada*?"

"Yes. But this is a special situation that involves the reputation of the brothers. I am respected and can get permission to take one man inside."

"What about you?" Rasmussen asked Nellie.

With a glance at Ortiz, she said: "Everyone out there knows me. Besides, any woman would be conspicuous. I'll stay at the hotel."

"Then, let's get to it," Rasmussen said, anxious to be doing something. "Every hour they're out of our sight, I'm afraid they'll vanish and we'll never find them again."

"That treasure is somewhere close by. You can depend on it," Thorne said. "If it's as big as rumored, it'll take a least a day for five men to load it, even if they're sitting right on top of it."

"Then what are they waiting for?" Nellie wondered aloud. "They've been out there a couple of days and nights already."

No one ventured an answer to this.

"Santiago will report to me this afternoon," Ortiz said. "Come to the store at four o'clock and I will disguise both of you. Those five *hombres* will not make a move that you do not know about."

Chapter Eighteen

A pounding on his hotel room door nudged Rasmussen gradually awake. He sat up, groggy and sweating in the afternoon heat, and swung his legs over the edge of the sagging bed.

Thorne was quicker and more alert. "Who is it?" he snapped, gun in hand.

"*Señor* Thorne . . . *Señor* Rasmoosen," came a childish voice. "*Señor* Ortiz wants you. Come quick!"

Thorne yanked open the door. It was the dark-skinned boy with the big eyes from the store.

"What's happened?" Rasmussen asked, grabbing his gun belt from the bedpost and buckling it on.

Thorne was pulling on his boots.

"Men come," the boy said, not venturing to enter the room.

"The men we want?"

"No. Others."

"How many?"

"Six."

"Anglos?"

"*Sí.*"

"Are they at the store?"

"*Sí. Señor* Ortiz send me out the back way to find you."

"What do they want?"

"They ask about the same men you came for."

Thorne and Rasmussen exchanged quick glances. The Claytons.

"You stay here while we go see," Thorne told the boy. He pointed at the adjacent room. "Knock and tell the *señorita* where we are."

"We need to get a look at them before they see us," Rasmussen said, following Thorne out the back door of the hotel. They skirted the rear of the buildings to approach the store.

The boy had left the door ajar and both men sidled up to it, hands on their holstered weapons. Rasmussen could hear movements inside, but no voices. They waited a long minute, but heard nothing further.

"Go around front and take a look. I'll stay here."

Rasmussen slid along the side of the building and put his eye to the corner of the front display window. Luis Ortiz was alone, in the act of lifting a metal washtub to the counter. Rasmussen stepped to the door and entered. Ortiz jumped and dropped the washtub with a clatter. He put a hand to his chest in relief.

"Ah, *Señor* Rasmussen!"

"Come on in, Alex!" Rasmussen called through the back room. "Where are they?" he asked Ortiz.

The storekeeper went to the window and pointed. "Down the street at the saloon. See? Their horses are at the hitching rail."

"Describe these *hombres*," Thorne said, moving up to the window.

"Six men. Riding new saddles on strong horses. They have fine guns and carry rifles in their scabbards."

"Any old men among them?"

"One. Fatter than me. Only a little white hair on his head."

"Walter Clayton," Thorne said.

"Did a small, dark, younger man have his right hand bandaged?"

"Bandaged? No. But such a one wore a large leather glove on one hand."

"Johnny," Rasmussen said. "I wouldn't know any of the rest."

"The other four are big men, hard-looking. The old man called one of them Rogers."

"Black Rogers," Rasmussen muttered, a chill running up his back at the thought of his would-be assassin only a half block away. He could still feel the back wound that had nearly cost him his life.

"They seek the same men you do," Ortiz went on.

"What did you tell them?"

"For them, I was a dumb Mexican who spoke little English. When I pretended to understand, I told them I knew nothing of such men."

"Did they believe you?"

"No. They threatened to kill me if I was lying. I did not have to pretend fear." He wiped a trickle of perspiration from his brow, a pallor showing through the dark skin.

Rasmussen could feel his anger rising at the treatment of this inoffensive Mexican. He glanced out the window again. "Maybe they're just having a few drinks before they move on," he mused. "It's too early in the day to make camp or get hotel rooms."

"No." Ortiz shook his head. "They spoke in front of me because they didn't think I understood. They believe the men they seek are close by. They will threaten anyone at the saloon to get information."

"And everyone in the village knows there are men camped at Tres Lobos Cañon," Thorne finished.

"So we can assume they'll head that way as quick as they find out," Rasmussen said.

"And they'll start shooting right off," Nellie said, entering the room from the back storeroom, the Mexican boy trailing behind. "They didn't come all this way just to negotiate. This has been building for a long time, and we're about to see the showdown." Her tone was firm and certain, as if she were relieved that all the uncertainty would finally be resolved. "The sniping is over," she continued. "The big prize is at stake here. However it turns out, I'll be glad to see the end of it . . . even if one side wipes out the other. At least it will be done."

"Is there a telegraph in Río Colorado?" Thorne asked Ortiz.

"No, *señor*. The nearest is in Santa Fé."

Thorne chewed on the corner of his mustache. "Give me a pad and pencil."

The storekeeper obliged, and Thorne leaned over the countertop and wrote out a message. He folded and handed it to Ortiz. "Is there someone trustworthy who can ride a fast horse to Santa Fé and get this to the Western Union operator at the depot there?"

"Blanco can do it," he said without hesitation.

"Blanco?"

Ortiz reached behind him and pulled the boy forward. "Blanco, saddle my best mare, and ride her slowly out of the village. Then ride like the wind to Santa Fé and take this paper to the telegraph man at the train depot." Ortiz pressed the message into the boy's hand. "You know where it is?"

The boy nodded, bright eyes even wider than before when Thorne added a small gold coin.

"Have the telegraph man send this. Wait for an answer. Then return here as quickly as you can, even if you have to trade my horse for another. Here, I'll give you a note to say that you have this horse with my permission and can do whatever you please with her."

The boy tucked both folded papers and the coin into a tight pocket of his jeans.

"Go now!"

Blanco vanished out the back door.

"Can the boy be trusted with such an important job?" Thorne asked.

"He is only twelve years old, but I would trust him over anyone else in the village," Ortiz said. "The boy has learned to survive many hardships. Two years ago he strayed into my care like a homeless, hungry Mexican puppy, and I named him Blanco after the Sierra Blanca."

"An odd name," Nellie said.

"The Yaqui Indians captured him in Mexico, then traded him to the Sierra Blanca . . . the White Mountain Apaches in Arizona. The boy told me a missionary gave the tribe several horses to release him to an orphanage. Blanco hated the strict white Christians as bad as he hated the Indians, so he ran away and hopped a freight train to Santa Fé, where I found him. I have tried to raise him as the son I did not have." He smiled. "He will do anything for me. He is a natural horseman, and weighs very little. The perfect one to take your message."

"They're coming out now," Rasmussen said, still watching through the window.

The others crowded up to see the horsemen mounting up in front of the saloon.

"They haven't been there long enough to get real drunk," Rasmussen said.

"You can bet old man Clayton wouldn't allow that. No more than two or three drinks to work up their courage."

"Looks like they got the information they were after," Thorne said as the six riders turned their mounts down between the buildings and headed west toward Tres Lobos.

"By the time we grab our horses and saddle up, they'll have a good head start on us," Rasmussen said, yanking open the front door.

A quarter hour later, Thorne, Rasmussen, and Nellie were ready to ride out after the six men. Ortiz put a *Closed* sign on his store, and, since Blanco had taken the only saddle horse, Ortiz slipped a hackamore on one of his two mules, threw a blanket on him, and vaulted aboard.

The four rode easily, not hurrying. The open country afforded a long view to the gap between the mountains that marked the mouth of Tres Lobos Cañon, several miles distant. Roiling dust showed the position of the Clayton party two miles ahead.

Fording the shallow Río Grande, the four continued westward at a leisurely walk. Eventually they lost sight of the rising dust ahead of them, and rode cautiously, keeping to the scant cover of the mesquite and desert scrub. Rasmussen strained to hear the sound of gunfire. Unless the Claytons had stopped, they should be at the Newburn camp by now.

The low, stone *morada* finally came into view, and the four rode to the side of it, keeping the building between them and whatever lay ahead. They dismounted.

"We can go inside the *morada*," Ortiz said. "There is a window on the other side where we can watch. . . ."

A sudden volley of gunfire blasted the afternoon stillness. Rasmussen's horse jumped, yanking the reins from his hand, and plunged away into the desert brush.

"Damn!"

The crashing fire died as suddenly as it'd begun. Thorne, Ortiz, and Nellie jerked their spooked animals to a hitching rail near the wall of the *morada*, tying them securely. The horses snorted, tossing their heads and walling their eyes.

"Follow me," Ortiz said, taking a key from a cord around his neck and unlocking a padlock on the door at the end of the oblong building. As they crowded into the dim interior, Rasmussen glanced in the direction from which the firing had begun again. He saw nothing.

Inside, the closed stone building, with the packed earthen floor, retained the damp chill of a cave. The *popping* of nearby gunfire was strangely muted. Ortiz slid the bar from the single window in the west wall, and swung open the wooden shutters. They crowded to the low, wide window, but there was little to see, even though the battle raged less than a quarter mile away. Sporadic movements caught their eye as one or another of the combatants shifted position in the desert washes 100 yards distant. Smokeless powder gave no indication of the shooters' positions, and the mid-afternoon sun allowed no muzzle flashes to be seen.

"Reckon they saw the attack coming?" Rasmussen muttered.

"Likely had a look-out posted," Thorne said, "or they'd have been cut down in that first volley."

The body of a dead horse lay in the open; the rider was nowhere to be seen. Everyone had gone to ground and the shooting settled into sporadic firing.

Rasmussen had a chance to get his first daylight look at the terrain; it was much different from the impression he'd gotten earlier.

In an open area, the hastily abandoned campfire still trailed a wisp of white smoke upward, then raveled away on a slight movement of air. The overturned black coffee pot lay on the ground; bedrolls were scattered nearby.

"Thought I saw a head over the edge of one of those freight wagons," Thorne said.

"One or two more of the Newburns are on the other side of the railroad embankment," Rasmussen added. "I saw the sun glint on a rifle barrel." He glanced at the railroad. "How many trains along this spur line?" he asked Ortiz.

"One goes north and one goes south each day."

"What time?"

Ortiz shrugged. "*¿Quién sabe?* They do not run on a schedule."

A rifle *cracked* from the far side of the embankment. It was answered by three shots from the Claytons—to no ill effect.

Rasmussen saw movement beyond the freight wagons. The backs of several mules were visible, tethered well out of harm's way.

"Beyond the tracks is Tres Lobos Cañon?" Rasmussen asked, pointing at the deep cleft between two brush-covered mountains.

"*Sí.*"

"What's that white spot on the side of the hill?"

"White and gray rock. It is the quarry I told you about."

Rasmussen was now oriented, and it appeared to his eye that neither of the warring parties had an advantage.

Twenty minutes dragged by with only an occasional shot being fired. Now and then a darting movement marked one of the Clayton party scurrying to a better vantage point. The six men and their mounts were scattered through arroyos carved in the desert floor after years of run-off from the nearby mountains.

"Hell, this could go on for a week," Rasmussen said, stepping back from the window.

"Maybe until dark," Thorne said. "Then the best guerilla fighters will win."

"Or the Newburns could slip out under cover of night."

"I doubt they'll do that. They didn't come all this way to run at the first attack," Thorne said.

Nellie nodded her agreement. "They'd have to leave the wagons behind, too," she added, then flinched from the window as a stray bullet struck close, spattering rock chips inside.

"Keep your head down," Thorne warned. "Nothing to see, anyway."

Ortiz struck a match to a coal-oil lamp. Its warm glow dispelled a little more of the interior gloom in the dank room.

Not expecting a protracted struggle, they hadn't brought food or water. To distract himself from his growling stomach, Rasmussen wandered about the room. There was little to see beyond a makeshift altar at one end, surmounted by a small cross. Two carved wooden *santos*, dark-visaged with pointed beards, adorned two niches in the wall.

"What's this?" Rasmussen asked Ortiz, picking

up a small model of a two-wheeled Mexican cart with a skeleton seated in it. The skeletal figure was holding a bow and arrow.

Ortiz hesitated, taking the model from his hand and replacing it on a small table. "This is a model of the death cart. *Los Hermanos* have a full-size cart like this that a penitent pulls in the Holy Week procession. Sometimes it is loaded with rocks to make it more difficult to pull. It reminds us to keep our own deaths constantly before our eyes. We must never lose sight of where we are bound."

Rasmussen nodded, wondering if a real human skeleton were used. Something of a morbid practice, he thought, akin to depictions of the Grim Reaper as a skeleton in a hooded cape, wielding a scythe. But, then, he wasn't about to judge someone else's cultural or religious practices.

Time began to drag as the stalemate outside continued. Now and then a shot or two punctured the afternoon stillness. Every few minutes Rasmussen checked the view from the window. Only the dead horse and the dying campfire were visible of what otherwise was a peaceful day. The sun beat down from a cloudless sky, and three black vultures appeared, wheeling on thermals high overhead, apparently attracted by the scent of death.

Another hour passed, and the inside of the *morada* grew warm and stuffy. Thorne propped open the end door to admit some fresh air.

"I will go back to the village and bring us food and water," Ortiz finally said.

"Good idea," Thorne said. "That way we can last as long as they can."

Rasmussen followed the storekeeper outside and unsaddled their rented mounts and tethered them closer to some browse. His own horse, that had bolted at the initial blast of gunfire, was cropping sparse grass nearby, and Rasmussen quietly gathered the dragging reins and tethered him near the same mesquite thicket.

Ortiz mounted his mule and rode away, keeping the stone building between himself and the stalemated gunfight.

An hour and a half later, Ortiz was back. He dismounted, tossing a sack to Rasmussen, who'd gone out to meet him.

"I have bread and cheese and jugs of water. Also a blanket for each of us, if we must sleep here tonight."

Apparently Ortiz had borrowed a saddle and bridle while in the village. He reached under the flap of the saddlebags and brought forth a fat bottle encased in wicker. "I even bring some very good red wine." He grinned like a mischievous boy on a camping trip.

Rasmussen was tempted to pull the cork and sample it right now, but knew he'd be asleep in a half hour if he did. He must keep his senses sharp in case something erupted in the quiescent battlefield in the brush beyond the *morada*.

He carried the food, jugs of water, and blankets inside while Ortiz followed with the wine. They all sat on the floor to eat, the men cross-legged, Nellie leaning back against the stone wall, munching on a piece of cheese.

They'd all been keyed for action, for some climactic ending to this situation, but now were somber and quiet as the Mexican stand-off continued.

"I reckon we ought to rotate the watch through the night," Rasmussen said to Thorne as the sun disappeared behind the mountain and the long summer twilight began to settle across the land.

"I'll take the first three hours," Thorne said, "then Ortiz and Nellie can each do a couple of hours. You take the pre-dawn guard. But we'll all be awake if something happens." He gestured toward the hidden gunmen. "Lying out there in the dust and sun all afternoon, they're ready to end this stand-off. I fully expect a few of 'em won't see the sun come up tomorrow."

Chapter Nineteen

Rasmussen had never been so glad to see the coming day.

With a blanket around his shoulders against the chill, he stepped out the end door and looked toward the eastern sky that was at long last beginning to pale slightly, allowing him to distinguish the ragged horizon and the outline of the hotel roof in the distant village. Thorne, Nellie, and Ortiz huddled in oblivion on the floor inside, wrapped tightly in their blankets.

Rasmussen felt dragged out by too little sleep. He'd been awake most of the night, half expecting gunfire or screams to erupt. But, unless there'd been some stealthy stalking and knife fighting, the night had passed peacefully. Would full daylight reveal more food for the buzzards? Or an abandoned battlefield?

Pacing slowly around the outside of the *morada*, he mentally savored the taste of a hot cup of coffee. He paused in the darkness to urinate, then moved to the end of the building, straining his eyes in a vain attempt to see what lay beyond to the west.

Dawn crept silently over the New Mexico landscape, graying the bushes, the tethered horses, the blocky *morada*. Objects could be now be distinguished, but the sun had not yet cleared the horizon.

The door to the *morada* opened and Nellie emerged, wrapped in a blanket.

"You're awake," he greeted her.

"Haven't slept much," she said, yawning. "Too cold." She hugged the blanket closely as Rasmussen moved up and put an arm around her shoulders.

"Want a drink of water?" she asked as he released her.

"Sure. I. . . ."

A scuffling in the mesquite nearby made him jump back and snatch his pistol. His heart pounded as he tried to make out the source of the noise. Probably some animal.

Hee-Haw! Hee-Haw!

The mule's raucous braying was followed by the voice of a man, cursing.

Rasmussen sprinted around the mesquite thicket, gun drawn.

"Hold it right there!" He thumbed back the hammer.

The man let go of the mule's headstall and lifted his hands.

Nellie came up from behind. Rasmussen heard her gasp: "DJ!"

The hatless man looked haggard in the pale morning light, deep pouches under his eyes. "Nellie?" His hang-dog face melted into a grin and he lowered his hands. "By God, what're you doing here?"

"Long story. Let's get you inside. You're hurt."

He glanced at his left shirt sleeve that was ripped to the shoulder. A blood-stained rag was crudely tied around his upper arm.

"Second time I've bled for the sake of that damned

gold," he muttered as they led him inside and closed the door.

"Got any water?" he asked, sagging against the wall.

Nellie handed him a jug and he tipped it up, taking a long drink.

"Needed that," he gasped, handing it back.

Ortiz and Thorne were awakened and gathered around.

"My cousin, Darrel Weaver," Nellie said. "He's one of us." She introduced the three men to DJ.

"What's going on out there?" Thorne demanded.

"The Claytons jumped us yesterday. Lucky we'd posted a look-out, or they would've finished us quick. Settled into a stalemate."

"We saw that much," Thorne said impatiently.

"We followed them out here and we've been watching," Rasmussen explained. "Anybody killed?"

"Not so far. Couple of minor wounds." He glanced at his own arm that Nellie was tending as they talked. She'd removed the piece of dirty undershirt that bandaged the small, purplish bullet hole in the outer edge of the triceps. She washed off the caked blood and poured wine on it.

"Where were you going just now?" Rasmussen asked.

"I'd had enough. Don't know what Nellie told you about me, but I'm not here because I want to be. Old Silas Newburn offered me a decent sum to come along, but it's gotten to the point where it's not worth it. He can keep his damned money, and I'll keep my life." He grimaced as Nellie bound his arm with a clean bandanna. "When I saw how things were going, I figured it was time to leave. Slipped away from the cover of the wagons while it was still dark, and started for the village. Saw the mule and figured to snatch him and ride as far as I could."

"Where is the treasure and why didn't you go after it a couple of days ago?" Thorne asked.

The young man looked at them, one at a time, amazement growing on his long face. "You mean it's still a secret? Thought everybody knew by now. It's right over there." He pointed west, through the unshuttered window. "In that quarry. Hidden in plain sight. Sunk in eighty feet of water."

"I'll be damned!" Thorne said.

"How did you plan to get it?" Rasmussen asked.

"Silas was here years ago and had it figured out. He knew there was no way anyone could retrieve rotted sacks and boxes of heavy metal from that depth by trying to snag it from a boat, even if a man knew exactly where to drop grappling hooks. The water had to be drained." He stopped to nod his thanks to Nellie for a hunk of cheese on bread she handed him. He tore off a mouthful and chewed like a starving man while Rasmussen waited impatiently for him to continue.

"That's a big body of water," Darrel finally went on. "Old Silas isn't an engineer, but he figured if dynamite were set at the right spots, the lower side of that rock basin would cave in, releasing all the water down the cañon and giving easy access to the submerged treasure." He shook his head. "Damned dangerous, though, for the man touching off the charges. More than a dozen small bundles of dynamite sticks with blasting caps are set into strategic points along that rock. Then all the fuses are twisted together into one that stretches two hundred feet.

Has to be long enough to give the fool who lights it a chance to get away before tons of rock and water come crashing down on him."

"You're saying that the charges have already been set?" Rasmussen asked.

"Yeah. Did it myself," he added with a hint of pride. "Had to have some help doublejacking holes in the rock to plant the dynamite. Told Silas I'd set the stuff but somebody else would have to light it."

"So that's why you've been out here all this time," Nellie said.

"Yeah." Darrel nodded. "Silas knew the noise would bring people from the village, so he was hoping a thunderstorm would come up to disguise the boom." He shook his head. "Nature didn't cooperate."

A distant shout interrupted, and they all went to the window. The yell came from someone hidden in a dry wash and was answered by a man on the Newburn side. The five in the *morada* were too far away to distinguish the words. But a minute later, a small man with a limp emerged from the brush, waving a white rag tied to a stick.

"Johnny!" Nellie said.

Rasmussen couldn't tell from the quiet intensity in her voice if it was meant as an expletive, or a lingering endearment.

A big man came slowly from behind a freight wagon and approached Johnny Clayton who held the flag of truce. They met in the clearing by the dead campfire.

The discussion took place out of earshot, with some pointing and nodding. Then the two men returned to their respective lines.

Ten minutes dragged by. Nothing could be seen or heard from either side.

"Wonder what that was all about?" Thorne finally said.

"Some kind of agreement," Rasmussen guessed.

"If so, it's the first compromise I've ever heard of," Nellie said.

"Not in their nature," Darrel agreed. "More likely a demand for surrender, or no quarter will be given."

Finally the unmistakable rotund figure of Walter Clayton moved out of the brush, Johnny Clayton following two steps behind. Moments later, a lean man approached from the opposite camp. The rising sun shone on the silver hair of Silas Newburn.

"That's Uncle Tad with him," Nellie said.

"The two patriarchs meeting face-to-face to work out a deal," Rasmussen said.

"Actually looks that way." Nellie's tone was incredulous.

Johnny Clayton and Tad Newburn came together and spoke briefly. They separated and each helped his boss out of his coat. The two old adversaries stepped forward and began to circle each other cautiously, fists at the ready.

"Oh, my God! They're going to fight!" Nellie cried. "This is ridiculous!"

"About as ridiculous as this whole damned feud," Darrel said.

Silas feinted, but the phlegmatic Walter didn't take the bait. The lean man shot a left jab to the face, followed by a quick, one-two to the body. The fat man kept coming, shuffling forward as Silas dodged and skipped around.

More than a minute passed before the pugilists

stopped feeling each other out and began to land
some blows. It was apparent Silas considered himself a boxer, with quick footwork and lightning jabs,
while Walter came shuffling in, flat-footed, not giving an inch, looking for a killer blow to end it in one
punch.

The men from both sides of the conflict began to
creep forward out of their hiding places to get a
closer look at the fun, forming a loose circle around
the perimeter of the clearing. But it was fun with a
purpose. Could this be a winner take all contest?

"Damn," Darrel breathed softly. "Those two old
fighting cocks think they've still got spurs."

The five of them went outside and moved forward
as well, staying hidden in the mesquite thickets. No
one even glanced their way, so absorbed in this spectacle were the eight men. By the time Rasmussen,
Thorne, Nellie, Darrel, and Ortiz had moved close
enough to view the contest clearly from the lip of an
arroyo, the backers of each fighter were cheering on
their champions. The old men were grimly serious;
something vital was at stake here. Had the patriarchs agreed to fight it out in one last, grand battle?

Rasmussen wondered if the loser and his entou-
rage would go home and allow the winner's side to
retrieve the treasure. Not likely. Whatever had been
agreed to, this truce would erupt in gunfire as soon
as the fight was over. He felt sure of it.

With their heads above the lip of the dry wash and
concealed by brush growing along the edge, the five
watched, fascinated by the wheezing combatants.

Walter's left eye was swollen shut from the jabs,
and he constantly wiped a forearm across his mouth
to clear the blood trickling from his nose.

Silas still circled, but slowly. His arms had apparently taken on a load of lead and were hanging at his sides, his mouth slack, chest heaving.

There were no knockdowns—no rounds called to give the fighters a chance to recuperate. They would fight continuously until only one remained standing.

A much heavier Walter Clayton couldn't land any telling punches on his constantly moving opponent. Silas was still sidling around, but had slowed until Walter saw his chance and, blocking a weak punch, tied up the lean man in a clinch. The two of them tripped and fell hard. They went down grunting, rolling in the dust, gouging, kneeing, biting each other's thumbs and ears. Dust powdered the sweaty fighters until they looked like two giant gingerbread men.

They punched and butted with ever-decreasing ferocity, until finally the two men slumped apart. Walter rolled to his hands and knees and attempted to stand up, but couldn't raise his bulk off the ground. His head hung down, mouth open, like a buffalo bull who's received his death wound. Silas, only his bloodshot eyes showing through a mask of dust and white beard, doubled up on his knees, and coughed until he gagged.

"One more punch will do for him, Walter!" somebody yelled.

"Come on Silas!"

"Don't give up now. Get up! You can do it!"

"Kick the shit out of that fat bastard!"

But the shouts of encouragement became sporadic and melted away to silence. Black Rogers looked at Johnny Clayton who was squatting on his haunches, holding Walter's coat. The two of them looked across at the Newburns. Tad Newburn, his father's second, glanced back at the two other men behind him, and then looked away, apparently unable to meet their eyes. The other three men on the Clayton side, eyes fixed on the ground, began to shuffle back toward their shelters in the dry washes.

An embarrassed silence followed.

Nellie slid down behind the lip of the arroyo, motioned for the men to follow her, and they retreated silently, carefully to the shelter of the *morada*.

"Most ridiculous spectacle I've ever witnessed!" Darrel spat to one side, grabbed the wicker-covered bottle of wine, and turned it up.

"That's what years of feuding amounts to," Nellie said.

"Gold fever, robbery, shootings, ambitious plans, hatred, greed, vengeance . . . it's all come to nothing," Darrel said, wiping his mouth with his shirt sleeve. "Two old weak men with the toes of their boots in their graves making fools of themselves. Everyone out there realized it, too."

"But the treasure is still here for somebody to take," Thorne said.

The words were hardly out of his mouth before the morning stillness was shattered by gunfire. They rushed to the window and saw the clearing deserted. Four black vultures flapped heavily away from the swollen body of the dead horse at the edge of the brush.

"The battle's on again," Rasmussen said. "And this time they won't stop until one side or the other's wiped out." He turned to Darrel. "Do the Claytons know the treasure's in the quarry?"

He shrugged. "Don't know, but I'd suspect so."

"Then we need to create a distraction. You got any ammunition for that Colt?" He pointed at the holstered pistol on Darrel's belt.

"Five in the chambers and this many more." He pulled a small handful of cartridges from his pants pocket.

"Enough. Thorne, what about you?"

The loops on his gun belt were over half filled with cartridges.

"And I've got about twenty," Rasmussen said.

"I left Otto's Thirty-Eight at the hotel," Nellie added. "Only five shots in it, anyway."

"What've you got in mind?" Thorne asked, frowning.

"The way both sides have been blasting away at each other since yesterday, they must be low on ammunition. The Newburn party had five men. Subtract Silas and Darrel, here, and that leaves only three. The Claytons had six. Old man Walter is out of the picture, so they're down to five. That's a total of eight fighting men left, and Darrel said two of them have minor wounds. We create a diversion, and the three of us should be able to get the drop on those eight, and arrest them."

"How do you plan to flush 'em all into the open at the same time?" Thorne asked.

"Tres Lobos Cañon slopes slightly out of the mountains toward the flatter land. Run-off is what created all those dry washes. I saddle two horses and have Darrel lead me around to that quarry at the mouth of the cañon." He fingered a stick match from his vest pocket and held it up. "It's time to reveal the treasure."

Chapter Twenty

Even with a bullet in his upper left arm, Darrel proved to be a good rider. He led Rasmussen in a half circle, two miles in length. They circumvented the shooting so as to be out of range of any stray lead, but still within earshot to retain a sense of direction. They rode up and down the broken terrain, often following the beds of deep arroyos until a shallow spot afforded egress for the horses.

The sun bore down from overhead when they drew rein downslope of the deep quarry. Rasmussen looked up at the high walls of Tres Lobos Cañon rising above on either side. The gray-white slash of exposed rock lifted its enormous wall above their heads, and only then did Rasmussen begin to appreciate the size of this quarry—and the amount of water it held.

They dismounted and tied the horses to small shrubs, then began climbing the scree and tumbled boulders to the level of water. It was a long, tiring climb with the sun beating down in the windless air. Sweat stung his eyes before Rasmussen reached the edge of the huge rock basin. If Darrel's arm was paining him, he never let on as he paused and pointed at the sweep of dark, still water.

"I've been told the water's as deep as the climb we just made. Wanted you to see it. Now, let me show you where I planted the dynamite, 'cause when she blows, the rock should fly up and out that way." He gestured. "The water'll come roaring out like last year's Johnstown flood. It'll cover everything down into the flats, but should dissipate before it reaches the village a few miles east on higher ground."

Rasmussen's gaze traveled down the steep incline and out through the mouth of the cañon across the sloping desert floor to the low stone *morada* in the distance. "Good thing we told Ortiz and Nellie to get on the roof."

"The force of the water will probably wash out the railroad embankment, but that can't be helped."

Rasmussen took a deep breath and steeled himself. "Then let's get to it."

Darrel led the way, angling down across the jumbled rocks, stepping carefully over the exposed fuses as he pointed out the places where he'd set the charges into the solid rock to keep from merely blowing loose boulders off the slope.

"You ever done anything like this before?" Rasmussen asked when they finally reached the last charge and were following the single, long fuse down to the bottom.

"Hell, no. You think I'm crazy?"

"Then how do you know it will work?"

"This is one of those things you can't practice. I convinced old Silas that I knew all about dynamite and had some experience." He turned his face up toward Rasmussen, squinting in the sun. "I lied."

Rasmussen grinned at his audacity.

"Figured if I was the dynamite man, I could somehow get out of defending that damned treasure in a showdown. Didn't work that way. Caught another slug, to go with the one I'm still carrying in my back." He sounded more disgusted than pained.

When they reached the bottom, Rasmussen was out of breath as much from nervousness as from exertion. Gunfire popped in the distance.

"This is a fast-burning fuse with a lot of imbedded powder to keep it from going out." Darrel picked up the loose end of the fuse as thick as his finger.

Rasmussen's gaze followed it upward until it disappeared over the tumbled rocks. Somewhere above, it connected to other fuses that were connected to the dynamite. Darrel had inspected each of these connections to be sure all of them were secure.

"We'll have to ride like hell," Rasmussen said.

Darrel nodded. "But not so fast that our horses might stumble in these rocks or step into a hole. I figure we have about ninety seconds from the time we light the fuse."

Rasmussen felt an icy lump in the pit of his stomach. They couldn't get a mile away in the rough terrain before the rock dam went sky-high.

Each untied his mount. Rasmussen felt for a match in his vest pocket.

"I'll light it," Darrel said.

"You shouldn't take the responsibility," Rasmussen demurred.

"Hell, we'll likely be dead in a few minutes. What difference does it make?" His hound-dog face melted into a sardonic grin.

Rasmussen still hesitated, holding the match.

"I've stopped two bullets defending this treasure. That gives me the right," Darrel insisted, holding out his hand.

Rasmussen couldn't argue with that. He handed over the match.

"Mount up and hold my horse," Darrel said.

Rasmussen swung into the saddle and took the reins.

Darrel squatted and struck the match on a stone, then held the flame to the end of the corded fuse. The black powder flared up. Smoking and hissing like a thing alive, the blaze snaked up the hill.

Darrel watched for five seconds to be sure it was burning properly.

"Let's go!" Rasmussen yelled, his horse prancing in a circle. Darrel vaulted into the saddle, and the two of them kicked their mounts into a dead run down the slope toward the bottom of the cañon. Ninety seconds! Maybe seventy by now, unwinding toward a minute. Rasmussen's heart was hammering as fast as the horses' hoofs.

Some white specks in the distance—shepherd's flocks! He'd forgotten about them. Then he realized they were uphill, at a safe distance inside the cañon on some grassy meadows. His horse leaped a shallow wash and Rasmussen was pitched forward, nearly losing his seat. He regained his balance and focused on guiding his mount. He turned slightly as Darrel came alongside.

"Uphill into the cañon!" he yelled.

Darrel shook his head emphatically. "Too steep for the horses!" he shouted back, pushing ahead.

Rasmussen could almost hear a pendulum in his head ticking off the precious seconds. He bent over the flying, brush-covered ground, praying he could react quickly enough to avoid any obstacles. The horses carried them at a full gallop down the gradual incline, and Rasmussen settled into the saddle with an easy, rocking motion.

But still they didn't seem to be gaining on the railroad that angled across in front of them a mile ahead. Engineers had notched the grassy embankment with a thirty-foot wide cut to allow rain and snow run-off to pass through into the desert beyond. Bridging this gap was a trestle of massive timbers. Darrel was riding to pass under this trestle to the relative safety beyond.

Over the sound of wind rushing past Rasmussen's ears came a deep rumble. Then the rest of the charges detonated nearly together with a *boom* like a blast of thunder, reverberating from the cañon walls. He dared not twist to look back as his horse's gait suddenly faltered when a shock wave shivered the ground. The animal seemed to be thrown off balance for a second, but quickly got his feet under him and plunged onward.

The grassy slope toward the railroad was open now and Rasmussen chanced a glance over his shoulder.

If he hadn't been so hard put at the moment, his heart would have stopped. Everything behind was blotted out by a billowing cloud of dust and smoke, rising into the sky. Like an erupting volcano, the cloud was raining rocks of all sizes. He faced about and leaned over the neck of his laboring horse, wind flattening the brim of his hat, ends of the flying mane whipping against his face. Pebbles began striking the ground around him, one cutting his wrist and another bouncing off the crown of his hat. He prayed the big boulders were falling short. Small rocks struck his horse's flank. The hail of sharp grapeshot spurred him to stretch his drumming stride.

Rasmussen glanced back once more. What he dreaded most was pursuing them like a giant dragon. A foaming wall of solid blue-green water had burst from the shattered quarry and came roaring down the cañon, whipping from side to side, carrying everything before it—boulders, bushes, trees. No horse on earth could outrun that monstrous cataract.

But the embankment was drawing closer. At the last second Darrel veered away from the gap under the trestle and let his horse's momentum carry him up the steep, grassy slope. Five seconds later Rasmussen's mount lunged up after him and both men turned their horses to the left, along the tracks. Rasmussen saw Darrel's reasoning—the eight-foot-high embankment would be little deterrent to the flood. They had to make a dash to one side, out of its path. The horses were slowing, their sides heaving like bellows. But they seemed to sense the danger and clods flew from straining hoofs as they carried their riders alongside the rail bed. Thank God the horses had firm footing, since there was no loose rock ballast on this spur line.

Glancing to his left, Rasmussen saw the rushing wall of water tumbling along its load of débris. Twenty seconds later it smashed into the railroad embankment. A huge wave spewed rocks and trees skyward, a second before the force of water carried away the embankment like piled sand. Tracks bent and disappeared under the onslaught that breached the puny obstacle. Trestle timbers floated away like twigs on the brown water that flooded down the valley, filling dry arroyos, spreading over the desert landscape.

Darrel and Rasmussen pulled up their lathered

mounts and jumped off, breathless, but safely above and to one side of the flood.

Exhilarated, heart pounding, Rasmussen raked off his hat, ran his fingers through his hair. He gazed at the tortured landscape that was awash in swirling, brown water. The flood circled the base of the stone *morada* in the distance before losing its momentum and spreading wide over the flats, quenching the thirsty desert. He couldn't see any horses or humans struggling in the water. Everyone below had certainly heard and seen the explosion. They would've had time to get away before the water cascaded down on them.

Above Tres Lobos Cañon the cloud of smoke and dust was shredded by a breeze, its remains drifting slowly off to the northeast. Except for the water still sluicing through the breach in the railroad embankment, an eerie silence had settled over the scene.

"It's almost like playing God," Darrel said in an awed whisper.

"Yeah. Thank God and these horses, we're still upright and breathing," Rasmussen said. "We better cool 'em down gradually." He took the reins and began walking along the right of way, leading his mount. Darrel followed.

After a few yards, Rasmussen's knees suddenly felt as if they were pivoting on greased ball bearings. Reacting to the shock of their narrow escape, he sank to the ground before he collapsed. "Let me just rest a minute," he said gruffly. "Here, walk my horse a ways. I'll catch up."

"Hell, I'm feeling pretty shaky myself," Darrel said, clinging to the saddle horn for support.

* * *

Like many desert flash floods, this one dissipated quickly, soaking into the wide flats, leaving fresh layers of mud and sand, small desert shrubs half buried, the arroyos cut ever deeper. But it still took more than an hour before Darrel and Rasmussen, leading their tired mounts, sloshed through hollows of knee-deep muddy water around the perimeter of the flood to the *morada*. Some three dozen curious villagers were scattered within a few hundred yards, gazing at the devastation and talking among themselves.

Rasmussen and Darrel found Thorne, Ortiz, and Nellie guarding Silas Newburn and Johnny Clayton. The two prisoners, wet and bedraggled, sat on two wooden boxes in the sun against the outside wall of the *morada*.

"Thank God you're both safe!" Nellie cried. She ran up and embraced Rasmussen. "I prayed for you," she breathed in his ear.

"Figured that was the way of it," Johnny sneered. "You were hoping I was drowned like a rat, so you could take up with that blond bastard. But I fooled you."

"Shut up, Johnny!" she snapped.

"Where are the rest of them?" Rasmussen asked. He had a flash of guilt for wishing Johnny had not been captured alive.

"Walter Clayton had an apparent heart seizure and drowned," Thorne answered. "According to these two, the rest of them managed to get to their horses and escape. From the roof, we saw a few riders scattering through the mesquite."

"You'll pay for killing my grandfather," Johnny said, black eyes venomous.

"He wanted the gold, and we exposed it for him," Darrel said lightly.

"You'll pay," Johnny repeated. He pushed back the wet, black hair plastered to his forehead. His oversize glove was missing and Rasmussen noted his reddened, bullet-deformed hand. "Hadn't been for this hand and my bad leg, I'd been able to snatch a horse and been gone."

"How many years will he get for robbery and kidnapping?" Rasmussen asked Thorne rhetorically for Johnny's benefit. "Maybe thirty?"

Silas Newburn stared silently into space, as if in shock. Normally fastidious about his appearance, his clothes were soaked, white beard streaked with red mud, eyes bloodshot, mouth slack. He looked every day of his seventy-eight years.

Rasmussen glanced at Nellie.

"He's been like that since we pulled him out of one of those half-buried wagons," she said, tears welling up in her eyes. "I know he's done a lot of bad things, but he's still my grandfather. I remember the good days when I was a little girl. He was always kind to me."

"Too bad Black Rogers got away," Darrel said.

"We don't know that he did," Thorne said. "He could be out there somewhere, buried under the mud."

"It's almost noon," Ortiz broke in. "We should go back to the village, get cleaned up, and eat. We can put this one on my mule," he added, pointing at Silas Newburn.

Everyone, including himself, Rasmussen noted, seemed to be reacting and talking very slowly, as if in a dream. He shook himself, hoping to wake from his lethargy.

"I know how you feel," Darrel said, evidently interpreting his action and manner. "We'll be all right when the shock wears off."

"You've still got a bullet in your arm," Rasmussen said.

"We do not have a doctor," Ortiz said. "But *Señora* O'Reilly, who runs the hotel, has treated many wounds. She has good, gentle hands and does much beautiful sewing. She will help you."

"Just what I need," Darrel said, rolling his eyes. "A seamstress."

Chapter Twenty-one

"Don't know that I'd do that, even for gold," Darrel said, looking down into the drained quarry at four local Mexican laborers, shoveling stinking, half dried muck.

It was four days later and Rasmussen, Darrel, Nellie, Thorne, and Ortiz stood on the upper lip of the old quarry supervising the removal of the long-hidden treasure.

As Rasmussen watched, a man pulled on a bag. The rotted leather ripped apart, and a golden shower of coins *jingled* over the Mexican's muddy boots.

"They're hired hands earning wages," Nellie said. "They won't get any of that gold. It means no more to them than shoveling gravel."

"Don't bet on it." Darrel laughed.

"They'll be searched before they leave the job each day," the ever-practical Thorne said, "just to make sure a few double eagles haven't fallen into the pockets of their overalls."

Rasmussen couldn't shake a feeling of unreality. From the time Nellie first told him of the treasure— and he finally believed her—he'd thought of it only in vague images, picturing it as the pot at the end of the rainbow, a vast and remote heaven of riches. Yet, here it was at his feet, covered with the muck and dross of earth, loot from everywhere dumped into the flooded quarry secretly by night over a period of more than twenty-five years.

The workers used coal shovels to scoop the silver and gold coins, jewelry and ingots into two makeshift sledges with foot-high sides. A mule was hitched to each, and, when loaded heavily enough, pulled the sledge to the lower edge of the quarry where the side had been blasted away. Another Mexican stood by to off-load the sledges and slide the load down a steep wooden flume laid over the jumbled rocks to a pair of heavy freight wagons below.

The wagons were guarded by two U.S. marshals, standing nearby with shotguns in the crooks of their arms. They were there because of the boy, Blanco, who'd ridden out of the village with Thorne's written message four days earlier. Blanco had made it to Santa Fé and paid Western Union to send it over the wire to the federal marshal service in Albuquerque. The reply had been immediate; the sender was instructed to wait at the depot for two deputy marshals to arrive. They'd loaded Ortiz's horse into a stock car, then Blanco had joined the marshals for the ride north on a passenger coach to within a quarter mile of the devastated trestle.

The boy was now struggling to adapt to the role of hero. A reporter, who'd been on the train, was taking down his story for the Santa Fé newspaper.

"He's the most famous man in the village," Ortiz said gravely, but with a sly grin. "I hope he doesn't take another job and leave my store."

"Speaking of jobs, are you still bent on becoming a Harvey Girl?" Rasmussen asked, guiding Nellie a few feet away to speak to her alone.

"Yes. I'm excited about it. I'm going down to Albuquerque and apply." She smiled at him. "Finally on my own, doing what I want to do."

He didn't know what to say. He had no claim on her. She was still legally married to Johnny, who would likely be in prison for a long time. To Rasmussen, the idea of divorce was distasteful, and one that she might not even consider. Besides, his mother and sister still awaited him—needed him—at least until their Minnesota farm could be sold for enough money to resettle them in town and have some extra cash in the bank. This adventure with Nellie had taken several weeks out of his life and left him only a couple of hundred dollars richer, after expenses. But love and money were two things he'd never been adept at acquiring.

"Once you get things settled at home, will you be back?" she asked, not looking at him.

"Yes, and it won't be just for the milder climate."

"If you come through on the train, I could be serving your dinner in the Albuquerque depot."

"We met over dinner in a Windsor hotel," he reminded her.

"That seems like a long time ago."

He nodded. "We've been through a lot since then."

They were silent for a few moments.

"Give me until September to get things settled," he said. "Meanwhile, if you want to write, send the letter to General Delivery, Champlin, Minnesota."

"Unless I give you a new address later, you can reach me at the Harvey House, Albuquerque," she said. "You won't forget me, will you, once you're back among all those beautiful Scandinavian blondes in Minnesota?" she added quickly.

He grinned. "I like brunettes. Small brunettes."

She smiled at him and they left it at that, both turning back to watch the treasure being retrieved from the muck below.

"It would seem more natural to see ore coming out of the mud, rather than minted coins and jewelry," Rasmussen remarked.

"*Whew!*" Darrel fanned himself with his hat. "Watching all that treasure shoveling has made my throat parched. I'm going to the saloon for lunch. Anyone coming with me?"

They all joined him, climbing carefully down over the tumbled boulders to their mounts below.

"A shame to see all that gold and silver get dumped into the maw of the federal treasury," Darrel said as he mounted up.

"Yes," Nellie agreed. "All this fighting and dying and suffering just so the United States government can take it all. Grandpa Silas has tried for years to get hold of it to fund his own new country," she said. "His whole dream vanished when he lost the cache. Besides, he's not in his right mind. I think he might've suffered a slight fit of apoplexy after that fight with Walter Clayton. Wonder if even a doctor could tell for sure?"

To Rasmussen she sounded weary, sad.

"But it might be best if Grandpa never comes out of it," she continued. "I doubt he could live with nobody to hate, now that old man Clayton is dead." She paused as the five of them urged their horses up and over the railroad embankment. The desert between them and the *morada* already looked as parched as if it'd been barren of water for weeks.

"My villagers have never seen anything like this," Ortiz said, gazing at the scattered groups of curious people who'd trekked several miles from town on horseback, afoot, and in wagons to view the flood's devastation and to glimpse the treasure that had lain on their doorstep for years.

"Wait'll the big Eastern papers pick up the story," Thorne said, "and the Denver and Río Grande repairs this spur line and trestle. This place will see another flood . . . this time of curious travelers."

"What will happen to Grandpa Silas?" Nellie asked.

"The two marshals will escort him and Johnny to jail in Santa Fé for now," Thorne said.

"But grandpa didn't do anything illegal," she insisted.

Thorne shrugged. "He'll probably be held for a short investigation and then released."

"I'll have to make sure Uncle Tad comes to look after him . . . if I can find Tad or Uncle Martin," she said. "No telling where they might have gone. They and Black Rogers and the others have scattered. Johnny'll probably go to jail for robbery, even if we never recover that quarter million dollars he took from me." She shook her head. "Who'd have thought things would turn out this way?"

"But maybe we've finally seen the end of this damned feud, Cousin," Darrel said, riding up alongside her. "As soon as my arm heals, I'll probably have to go back on the road, selling, since Silas is in no condition to pay me for trying to grab this treasure. I'd like to live near some of our kin in Missouri again, but not until I'm sure things have changed and I can get a decent job without working for the Claytons."

"Darrel, you and Nellie and Rasmussen and Ortiz were each indispensable to the successful conclusion of this operation," Alex Thorne said. "All of you will be amply rewarded for your services to the government." He sounded very sure of himself.

They all looked expectantly at Thorne.

"No one has any idea how much that cold cache is worth," he went on. "Millions. And the numismatic value of certain coins, I expect, will increase the total even more. It'll take months for appraisers to sort it out and come up with a figure."

They rode slowly in silence for a few seconds, the hot noon sun beating down on them.

"As I said, each of you played a vital rôle," Thorne said slowly, deliberately. "Therefore, in justice, you should be rewarded . . . without having to wait for years for your claims to go through the bureaucracy, then likely being denied by some hard-headed judge."

Thorne reined his horse to a stop, took off his hat, and squinted at them in the sunlight. A light breeze ruffled his salt-and-pepper hair.

The other four pulled up, sidling their mounts around to face him. Rasmussen knew the Secret Service man had something on his mind.

"I volunteered the four of you to help me guard the quarry tonight so the marshals could have the night off and get a good sleep," Thorne told them. "As tired as I am, I'm likely to doze off," he went on. "If I should be unable to keep my eyes open for a couple of hours, I don't want to wake up and see any mud on your hands, feet, or clothes. Do all of you understand what I'm saying?" He searched their faces, one by one.

They understood.

About the Author

Tim Champlin, born John Michael Champlin in Fargo, North Dakota, graduated from Middle Tennessee State University and earned a Master's degree from Peabody College in Nashville, Tennessee. Beginning his career as an author of the Western story with *Summer of the Sioux* in 1982, the American West represents for him "a huge, ever-changing block of space and time in which an individual had more freedom than the average person has today. For those brave, and sometimes desperate souls who ventured West looking for a better life, it must have been an exciting time to be alive." Champlin has achieved a notable stature in being able to capture that time in complex, often exciting, and historically accurate fictional narratives. He is the author of two series of Westerns novels, one concerned with Matt Tierney who comes of age in *Summer of the Sioux* and who begins his professional career as a reporter for the Chicago *Times-Herald* covering an expeditionary force venturing into the Big Horn country and the Yellowstone, and one with Jay McGraw, a callow youth who is plunged into outlawry at the beginning of *Colt Lightning*. There are six books in the Matt Tierney series and with *Deadly Season* a fifth featuring Jay McGraw. In *The Last Campaign*, Champlin provides a compelling narrative of Geronimo's last days as a renegade leader. *Swift Thunder* is an exciting and compelling story of the Pony Express. *Wayfaring Strangers* is an extraordinary story of the California Gold Rush. In all of Champlin's stories there are always unconventional plot ingredients, striking historical details, vivid characterizations of the multitude of ethnic and cultural diversity found on the frontier, and narratives rich and original and surprising. His exuberant tapestries include lumber schooners sailing the West Coast, early-day wet-plate photography, daredevils who thrill crowds with gas balloons and the first parachutes, tong wars in San Francisco's Chinatown, Basque sheepherders, and the *Penitentes* of the Southwest, and are always highly entertaining.

The Classic Film Collection

The Searchers by Alan LeMay

Hailed as one of the greatest American films, *The Searchers*, directed by John Ford and starring John Wayne, has had a direct influence on the works of Martin Scorsese, Steven Spielberg, and many others. Its gorgeous cinematic scope and deeply nuanced characters have proven timeless. And now available for the first time in decades is the powerful novel that inspired this iconic movie. (Coming February 2009!)

Destry Rides Again by Max Brand

Made in 1939, the Golden Year of Hollywood, *Destry Rides Again* helped launch Jimmy Stewart's career and made Marlene Dietrich an American icon. Now available for the first time in decades is the novel that inspired this much-loved movie. (Coming March 2009!)

The Man from Laramie by T. T. Flynn

In its original publication, *The Man from Laramie* had more than half a million copies in print. Shortly thereafter, it became one of the most recognized of the Anthony Mann/Jimmy Stewart collaborations, known for darker films with morally complex characters. Now the novel upon which this classic movie was based is once again available—for the first time in more than fifty years. (Coming April 2009!)

The Unforgiven by Alan LeMay

In this epic American novel, which served as the basis for the classic film directed by John Huston and starring Burt Lancaster and Audrey Hepburn, a family is torn apart when an old enemy starts a vicious rumor that sets the range aflame. Don't miss the powerful novel that inspired the film the *Motion Picture Herald* calls "an absorbing and compelling drama of epic proportions." (Coming May 2009!)

To order a book or to request a catalog call:
1-800-481-9191
Books are also available at your local bookstore, or you can check out our Web site **www.dorchesterpub.com**.

Paul Bagdon

Spur Award-Nominated Author of
Deserter and *Bronc Man*

Pound Taylor had been wandering the desert for days, his saddlebags stuffed with stolen money from an army paymaster's wagon, when he came upon Gila Bend. It was a wide-open town without law of any kind, haven to gunslingers, drifters and gamblers. Pound might just be the answer to a desperate circuit judge's prayers. He'll grant Pound a complete pardon on two conditions. All Pound has to do is become the lawman in Gila Bend. . . and stay alive for a year.

OUTLAW LAWMAN

ISBN 13: 978-0-8439-6015-0

"When you think of the West, you think of Zane Grey." —*American Cowboy*

ZANE GREY

THE RESTORED, FULL-LENGTH NOVEL, IN PAPERBACK FOR THE FIRST TIME!

The Great Trek

Sterl Hazelton is no stranger to trouble. But the shooting that made him an outlaw was one he didn't do. Though it was his cousin who pulled the trigger, Sterl took the blame, and now he has to leave the country if he wants to stay healthy. Sterl and his loyal friend, Red Krehl, set out for the greatest adventure of their lives, signing on for a cattle drive across the vast northern desert of Australia to the gold fields of the Kimberley Mountains. But it seems no matter where Sterl goes, trouble is bound to follow!

"Grey stands alone in a class untouched by others." —*Tombstone Epitaph*

ISBN 13: 978-0-8439-6062-4

COVERING THE OLD WEST FROM COVER TO COVER.

Since 1953 we have been helping preserve the American West
with great original photos, true stories, new facts,
old facts and current events.

True West Magazine
We Make the Old West Addictive.

TrueWestMagazine.com
1-888-687-1881

✂ ☐ **YES!**

Sign me up for the Leisure Western Book Club and send my FREE BOOKS! If I choose to stay in the club, I will pay only $14.00* each month, a savings of $9.96!

NAME: _____

ADDRESS: _____

TELEPHONE: _____

EMAIL: _____

☐ I want to pay by credit card.

☐ **VISA**   ☐ **MasterCard**   ☐ **DISCOVER**

ACCOUNT #: _____

EXPIRATION DATE: _____

SIGNATURE: _____

Mail this page along with $2.00 shipping and handling to:
Leisure Western Book Club
PO Box 6640
Wayne, PA 19087

Or fax (must include credit card information) to:
610-995-9274

You can also sign up online at **www.dorchesterpub.com**.

*Plus $2.00 for shipping. Offer open to residents of the U.S. and Canada only. Canadian residents please call 1-800-481-9191 for pricing information.

If under 18, a parent or guardian must sign. Terms, prices and conditions subject to change. Subscription subject to acceptance. Dorchester Publishing reserves the right to reject any order or cancel any subscription.

03/2020

GET 4 FREE BOOKS!

You can have the best Westerns delivered to your door for less than what you'd pay in a bookstore or online. Sign up for one of our book clubs today, and we'll send you 4 FREE* BOOKS, worth $23.96, just for trying it out...with **no obligation to buy, ever!**

Authors include classic writers such as
LOUIS L'AMOUR, MAX BRAND, ZANE GREY
and more; plus new authors such as
**COTTON SMITH, JOHNNY D. BOGGS,
DAVID THOMPSON** and others.

As a book club member you also receive the following special benefits:
- **30% off all orders!**
- **Exclusive access to special discounts!**
- **Convenient home delivery and 10 days to return any books you don't want to keep.**

Visit **www.dorchesterpub.com**
or call
1-800-481-9191

There is no minimum number of books to buy, and you may cancel membership at any time.
*Please include $2.00 for shipping and handling.